To Robert

Enjoy the third story

Lynn

Lurick

Copyright © 2023 by Lynn Luick

ISBN: 978-1-77883-141-6 (Paperback)
        978-1-77883-142-3 (Hardback)

All rights reserved. No part of this publication may be reproduced, distributed, or transmitted in any form or by any means, including photocopying, recording, or other electronic or mechanical methods, without the prior written permission of the publisher, except in the case brief quotations embodied in critical reviews and other noncommercial uses permitted by copyright law.

The views expressed in this book are solely those of the author and do not necessarily reflect the views of the publisher, and the publisher hereby disclaims any responsibility for them.

BookSide Press
877-741-8091
www.booksidepress.com
orders@booksidepress.com

Contents

Chapter 1 1
Chapter 2 9
Chapter 3 20
Chapter 4 30
Chapter 5 47
Chapter 6 57
Chapter 7 70
Chapter 8 83
Chapter 9 93
Chapter 10 106
Chapter 11 119
Chapter 12 130
Chapter 13 144
Chapter 14 156
Chapter 15 167
Chapter 16 178
Chapter 17 191

1

The day was hot with the sun beating down on us as we kept on moving across this hot dry desert of a wasteland. Our hats didn't protect us much for the sun seemed to burn right through to our heads and the dust made it through our handkerchiefs like they weren't tied around our faces. The sweat burned our eyes as it rolled down from under our hatbands. Foster, BJ and me had made it this far from our ranch. We were now walking for we had shared our last water with Blacky, Lagger and Red with the mule tied down with the heaviest load but that was two days ago and they were now tired as we were. Blacky and me had been together a long time and I was determined not to let him, Lagger or Red die like this. That takes me back to when Josh started his horse ranch. We rounded up around a thousand wild mustangs and we put Blacky in with a pasture of mares and Red was the first foal stallion born from that bunch. That is when Josh turned to BJ;

"He's yours son when he's winged from his mother. Just say it's a present for all the help you've given me." That takes me to thinking about Red Bird when I told her I was taking BJ with us on our trip. Why she had a fit, been with the whites to long but I told her he was now eighteen and what would her father, Dancing Bear say. She looked hard at me and said;

"You are right my husband; my father would have made him a warrior long before this. He will go with you. I forgot a boy must become a man. It is past time." The heat brought me out of my reverie.

Seems the army was having trouble with the Mescalero's getting rifles from somewhere down here around the border with Mexico. They couldn't legally go across the border into Mexico without starting a war. Every time the army came close to the band of Mescalero's on our side of the border, they were believed to be under Chief San Juan that lived in northern Mexico after leaving the reservation and now sometimes raided into Arizona and New Mexico, they would retreat back to Mexico. General Cook came to my ranch in Durango because of my dealings with Geronimo and the Delta Gang during our first cattle drive up north and convinced me to help the government find out where they were getting the repeating rifles and where they disappeared every time the army got close.

Of course Red Bird tried to talk me out of coming on this "fool trip" as she called it. Then my parents and most of the men tried to convince me not to come. They seemed to have remembered the trouble on the cattle drive. But Foster was the one that came to me at the last minute and insisted on coming.

"This town is just getting to tame and I'se want one more adventure before I'se part this world." That is the way he put it to me. I thought Blacky was too old to travel this far but on the morning we were leaving he up and jumped over the pasture fence and came trotting down the road after us so I went back and threw on his saddle that Foster had made and we were on our way like the old days of finding silver but this time BJ was beside us on Red. Just the six of us out on the trail with Foster's new mule Josephine tagging behind.

"This here is hotter than Hyades and just as barren."

"I guess you should know in your old age."

"Now Buck, don't you'se get smart with me'se."

BJ took to laughin' and I was laughin' as I continued.

"Alright but not much else to do to keep my mind off this fix we're in except those tall funny lookin' cactus out there. They must be trees of the desert but they don't make much shade to get cool under."

"We'se sure do need a drink. Look at those rocks over there, I'se think we'se should lay in that shade and rest till night then travel in the coolness under the stars."

The boulders were big enough to cast a long shadow for us to rest after we unloaded the mule. We couldn't make any coffee with no water but we could eat but there wasn't any firewood anywhere in our sight just some fallen down dead cactus. So I thought why not and gathered up some and struck a match to them and they burst into flames and we had our dinner. Sitting there eating I noticed that the cactus had some bubbles oozing out of the cracks in the plants as they became hotter.

"Look Foster, sure do wish that was water coming out of that burning plant."

"You'se know years ago when me'se and Jeb uses to partner up we'se ran across an old timer that came out of the desert. Mind you we'se were young back then but he said that you'se never could die of thirst out here cause of the cactus but never told us more."

"Do you suppose he meant something in the cactus that's all over this place for miles?"

I got up and took my knife out of its sheath and cut deep into one of the tall cactus, must had been twenty-five feet tall. That deep gash had liquid coming out all over my knife and then my fingers as I put my hand under the gash. I put my fingers to my mouth and took a taste.

"What you'se do that for Buck? Might be poison or something worse."

A smile came across my face as the taste reach my taste buds on a fast track to my brain.

"Not bad at all even a little tasty but it sure is wet."

I cut huge pieces off the plant and shaved off the thorns and cut it up in small pieces and fed it to Blacky but he just looked at it till I put it to my mouth and squeezed the oozing liquid over my scorched lips and down my parched throat. I again put some to his mouth and he took a bite and then another. Lagger and Josephine and Red too saw this and came forward and got a share. I put some more in my mouth and licked my lips as it went down. This brought Foster and BJ over.

"Well, all of you'se ain't dead so I'se guess I'se have some." BJ spoke up.

"Here let me cut some of that tall cactus down to size."

He uncoiled his fifteen-foot black bullwhip, that he had made while working for Foster in his leather shop and went to work with the sound of that whip cracking in the dry air had that cactus cut into small pieces in about five minutes.

"You'se know Silver that boy is a wonder with that whip I'se glad I'se put him to work when I'se did."

"You know he's also nearly as fast with that six-gun on his hip as pa and me."

The cactus burned well after we squeezed the thick watery liquid out so we had some dinner along with the sweet watery liquid to drink.

Everything around us took on a different hue and I could see the true beauty of this dry and desolate place. There were small flowers blooming at the end of truly wonderful plants and then I saw a small cactus plant with a small red apple looking fruit on top and took a small bite and it was like God's nectar. The horses chewed them up as fast as I put them to their mouths but stopped or they might keel over from eating to many. Apples had always been Blacky and Lagger's favorite.

We tried to sleep the rest of the day and then with the beautiful colored sky as the sun fell under the horizon in the west I woke to a coolness in the air that took my mind back to the mountains of my home. We ate and squeezed some of the cactus juice into our mouths and canteens then the horses and mule ate their fill. I went out in the lead for I knew Blacky could make a trail in total darkness and we were in twilight as the stars started to shine in the sky one by one as the night closed in around us. Then about three hours later a slit of a moon came out and gave us a little more light to see by. I knew we were in New Mexico and heading for the border but didn't know where exactly the border was or how far we had to tract to be in Mexico. We were riding now into the dark, refreshed by the coolness of the night and some moisture down our throats. By the small amount of light of the moon I could make out some mountains protruding up to the sky to the south so we took a more westerly course. These mountains weren't like the mountains of Colorado or Wyoming but I could tell we were higher in altitude but it was still flat land all around us except for the protruding mountains or hills compared to the mountains we knew. Then we would come to dry gullies and they remained in my mind in case we needed cover from pursuit and there was a few dozen we had to traverse. As we came close to the mountains I could see they were wider than first thought and there were trails turning into canyons that went who knows where.

"Buck, where do you'se thinks those canyons lead to."

"Well, only one way to find out and it may be a good place to spend another hot day. Plenty of shade and cover." I said as I turned Blacky into the first canyon and moved on.

"I'se hope no one is on our trail cause it is plain as day which way we'se heading."

But in short order BJ took care of that with his bullwhip and some time.

The sun was starting it's trek across the eastern sky by the time we found a ledge overhang made of solid rock that made a perfect place to sleep and rest the horses out of the heat of the sun and the canyon seemed to have a cool breeze coming off the top of the mountain. That coolness may not last long but for now it was great. The only downside was that the cactus had all but disappeared from this area so I walked in search of a large area around us to get enough juice for the animals and us and let Blacky rest. On my way back to camp I took another way to see and get to know this canyon and I had a tarp that I drugged behind me with all of the cut cactus that was to be found. I saw a small mound off to the north that was not the direction I was heading but there seemed to be something different on top of this mound so I headed toward it. I knew that Foster had breakfast ready by now but there was a feeling in me that told me to check this out.

As I neared the mound there was some kind of long blob on top and I could see hands and feet attached to stakes with leather thongs that looked to be tied really tight but no face or body was in sight until I got closer. I let go of the tarp and ran to the mound that I could tell were ants swarming all over something that I knew had to be a man. I went in fast and started grabbing hands full of ants and throwing them off the man that I now saw. The ants were now mad and were stinging me but I had to wait. The man's face was covered but I managed to get them away from his face and out of his eyes which were swollen shut then I got most of the ants from his body. Then grabbing my knife I cut the leather thongs and got my hands under his arms and dragged him off of the mound and far away from the ants. Then I was working over him getting the remainder of the ants from his body and mine. I saw a rock some fifty feet away so I heaved him over my shoulder and took him to the shade and away from the last of the ants. As I laid him down I could see he was naked from head to toe and his body was swollen and near burnt to a crisp from being out in the sun for who knows how long. He had long hair with a band around his forehead and his mouth was slightly open. I felt his chest and his heart was barely beating. I got some cactus and squeezed some juice into his open mouth. As I looked closer I could see someone had cut out his tongue. This looked to be the work of Indians but why would they do this to their own kind. Maybe Foster would know what to do for him so I made room for him on the tarp full of cactus then covered him up as best I could and started in the direction of camp but he was heavy and it was slow going. This sure wasn't the rest I should have been getting but I felt this was a good deed that would pay off in the next few weeks. Sweat broke out all over my body which made the ant bites burn and hurt worst as I pulled into sight of the camp and then Foster and BJ spotted me and the way I was moving they knew I had more than cactus on the tarp. They came running with the mule and we got the ends of the tarp attached to the mule and we made it the last hundred feet to camp under the shade.

"What you'se pick up out there that is this heavy?"

As my breathing came back to me I told him.

"Look at him he was tied to an anthill and is still alive but barely as I could tell and they cut out his tongue. Thought you might know what to do."

"Pa, the ants bit you."

"This is nothing compared to him."

As Foster pulled back the tarp his eyes enlarged as he saw all the stings and blisters from the ants and sun. They had done terrible harm to this human being.

"We'se have no water, I'se have to use the cactus juice for him. We may not get any more; sure you'se want me'se to do this he'll probably die anyways. I'se never seen anyone this bad off and live. Buck, this I'se think is a Mescalero Apache."

"Try Foster." I said and fell back on the ground in exhaustion and fell to sleep.

The minute I woke the pain hit me from pulling the Mescalero to our camp along with all the ant bites. My muscles were like knots in a rope. To move was pain but move I be bound to do for there was work to do and the ant bites I would just have to live with for a while. It was sure that someone wanted this man dead and we might have stopped him from dying so we had to assume that we would be hunted to if they found out. Foster had breakfast on as I went over to see how the Indian was doing.

"How is he doing?"

"I'se did what could be done but he's still bad off. Getting him out of the sun was good but we'se need water in him. His insides must be near as bad as the outside. That cactus juice doesn't do much for a man that's near dead. His mouth is bad and we'se won't get any food down him till that mouth heals."

"They sure did a job on him but we have to try. You get some sleep he won't be going anywhere and BJ and me are going to look for water in the rocks above here."

"Be careful cause the one's that did this may come back to make sure he's dead."

"I was thinking the same thing. I'll take Blacky and your canteen."

As we left camp it was sure we wouldn't be moving any time soon if he lived so we had to have water for us and the animals if we were going to go any further. We left Blacky and Red at the foot of the rock formation and went up into the boulders of rocks hoping to find just a trickle of water coming up from the rocks and I also needed to keep my eyes on the horizon for anyone that looked dangerous. The hours went by and still no luck as we moved from formation to more formations. From the look of the sun no water seemed possibly from up above. The area in this canyon was as desolate as I had ever seen. The red dirt on the floor of the canyon was as fine as dust and the red dust was all over the rocks and what bushes there were, giving everything a red tint. The only moving things besides us were some prairie dogs and lizards to be seen rarely scampering from rock to rock and back in their holes to get away from the scorching rays of the sun and our feet till the night would come over this desert and with the night the coolness. We were searching for water till the rays of the sun started to disappear behind the mountains in the west.

"Pa, who could have done that to him and why?"

"That is a good question and right now there is no answer. Maybe if he lives and can somehow communicate with us we might find out."

Then as I was standing on the pinnacle of rocks I spotted a lone rider leading a horse behind so I hit the rock flat as I could and told BJ to do the same with my rifle in hand hoping not to be seen.

2

As we looked closer it had to be an Indian woman with the long black hair flowing down the back all the way to the waist and the buckskin dress split nearly to the waist and the bare legs with moccasins on the feet with no saddle on either horse just blankets across the backs. But most of all was the movement of that slim full bosom body as the horse galloped across the canyon. I knew cause I had seen that movement enough times when watching my beautiful wife Red Bird riding across our ranch. Scanning behind her it was plain to see that she was alone and looking for something. Making it down to where Blacky and Red was and into the saddles moving toward the lone woman rider.

As we gain on her she turned around and spotted us so she put the horses at full gallop. This was hard on Blacky with not having any water for days but I had to know what she was looking for. As we came closer I could tell she was following the canvas marks I had made taking the Indian back to camp and that was just where she was heading. As I came up beside her I grabbed the rope of her horse and Blacky pull up as we came to a stop. She came off the horse and was running for the closest boulder as I caught her from behind and pulled her down on the ground. She was kicking and screaming so I had to straddle her and pin her arms to the ground. Her breasts were heaving with fright and I could see the panicked look in her deep dark black eyes. I looked in those eyes.

"Take it easy girl. I'm not going to hurt you. You look like you were looking for something and my son and I just wanted to try to help."

"Me no need white man's help. Let me up."

"You speak English. I'll let you up if you don't run away. We just want to help."

She looked into my eyes and spoke clear, unafraid and calmer now.

"You speak truth I not run away."

I got up off her and took her small strong hand in mine and pull her up off the ground.

"Horse fast as wind. My horse never caught that easy."

"Blacky would have caught you sooner but he hasn't had water for days now. We have been living off cactus juice. I was out looking for water when I spotted you but had no luck."

She walked to her horse and brought a skin bag to me.

"Water, you and son drink give horses. Cannot live long out here without water. I know more water."

I took the water and filled my hat and let Blacky and Red have their fill then we drank.

"Smart man give horse first he one get you out of this place."

"Now what you looking for? You were following the tracks I left yesterday."

"You find my man?"

She turned and pointed to the northwest.

"Yes, I did but he's in bad shape. Now I'm glad we saved him seeing he has a wife."

"Came to bury him thought dead by now. They not let me come till now. Brought horse to bury beside him so he would have horse to ride in happy hunting ground. When saw ropes cut knew he may be safe. Me make two graves so they think he dead and horse."

"They won't come and dig him up."

"They come but not dig. They are afraid of sprites. Now can we go to my man?"

"I'm sorry he's right over under that ledge in the shade."

By this time Foster came running from camp out of breath and the girl passed him on the way to the shaded ledge.

"Who's that! another Mescalero?"

"That's her husband I take it. She came looking for him. She thought he was dead by now."

"He nearly is but I'se see some improvement in him, just a little. We'se better get back we'se don't know what she means to do to him."

"Here's some water for you and the two animals. We had our fill. She gave it to me."

"Where she gets the water?"

"I didn't have time to ask." Talking to Foster as we rushed back to camp.

As we got closer we could see that she was looking over the Indians whole body. As we came up to her, she told us.

"Me give Peco water, you drink all you can. Me, you go get more. Take all animals to water. I look for plants to make Peco better. Hurry!"

"How far is the water?" I asked as we all drank the water after she poured a cup full.

"Not far. Need be careful might see Victorio. He bad if find Peco alive. Give Peco water far apart. Now you, me go fast."

"BJ, you stay here and help Foster."

"Yes. Pa."

We mounded and were gone into the desert, where to I knew not but she lead her extra horse and I lead the mule, Lagger and Red. She didn't slow her pace till she spotted something. She stopped and jumped off and pulled up a plant and flung it across her horse as she jumped back on and we were off again. This went on for an hour and then she stopped and got off again and looked at the ground then mounted.

"They not in here we can go through. Must be careful they might come any time." Then she worked us through a narrow crack in the boulders, as the canyon seemed to come to a dead end. We went along for a couple hundred yards with our legs rubbing the rocks on both sides and the rocks over our heads was blocking out most of the sun. Then there was some bright daylight coming into sight as we broke out into a valley surrounded by huge boulders but unlike the desert the ground was covered with lush green grass. Then I spotted the cottonwood trees that seemed to be growing out of the rocks. As she stopped under the huge trees with shade being cast for twenty feet the horses started grazing on the green grass that they hadn't seen for a long while. She pulled up more plants and moved some rocks from the base of the trees and there flowed water out forming a small pool at the feet of the cottonwoods.

This was like a calling card to the horses as they quit grazing and came to drink. This woman of the desert lay down on her stomach at the edge of the pool and drank and I didn't have to wait for an invitation did the same. The horses went back to the grass and when I got my fill I got the canvas off Blacky and handed it to her.

"Use this to gather more plants you might need for Peso and I will carry it on Blacky. My name is Buck Taylor and my friend is Foster and my son is BJ short for Buck Junior."

She took the canvas and gathered more plants as I followed her.

"Name is Solie. Plants will help make ants stings go away and make better. Take long time. Must hurry before braves come. See you have bites to rub some this plant on bites and be gone no time."

I looked over and the horses were at the water's edge again. I went and got the bag the girl had come in with and our canteens with another container I had brought for water. She dammed up the water and we mounted after I rubbed the plant all over my neck and arms where most of the ant bites were.

"This way, we hide here braves come. No sound, keep horses quiet."

She showed me another crack and pointed for me to take the horses in then she backed her horse in. I came to the end and waited. I could barely see out from where I was but I saw as six Indians passed and went to where the water was. We watched as they looked around where the pool of water had been. I then knew they had seen our tracks but as I looked where we came in this crack it could be seen that the lush grass had sprang back up leaving no sign of our passing. But the Indians were still not satisfied and separated to search the area. One brave stayed to open the flow of water. Thank goodness they didn't look to long for they wanted water and the horses smelled it. We heard them talk but I didn't catch every word cause they spoke Spanish and I only knew some from hearing Manuel, Juanita and Carlos around the ranch. They seemed to have forgot about searching any more for when they drank their fill and the horses drank they were gone as fast as they came in.

Solie spoke. "Me go out, make sure gone. Come on slow. They gone we hurry back."

She went out leading her other horse and I waited till she was out of sight and moved out slowly. As I reached the pasture of green grass I spotted her across the way and I turned as I heard a noise to my right and as I looked Blacky's ears stood up and a deer came bounding out of the glade along the wall of the canyon. I saw Solie enter the crack where we came in and I followed. As I entered there was no noise all the way through the dark. When I came out into the light I saw Solie waving for me. She pointed north and then took off south so I was right behind her as we came out of the canyon on to the desert floor. She wasted not a single second getting back to camp. She finally slowed to give the horses a rest and I rode up beside her.

"Do you know what they were talking about back there?"

"Say, Peso dead and I gone. Do not care where I go. Think me at water hole. Why not search any more. To my people I outcast now cause my man dead. Go back to village."

She galloped away again and we were in camp in an hour. She grabbed the canvas and dragged it to where Peso was and went to work with no thought of her needs. I got the water off the horses and put it out of the sun by Peso then walked over to Foster and BJ.

"We saw six braves but they didn't see us. There is a pretty little pasture with plenty of water and grass just a two-hour ride from here in a hidden valley. I couldn't believe my eyes."

We ate and now had water and I took Solie some food but she refused saying.

"Me take care of man, eat later."

I sat nearby and watched Solie as she took care of Peso. She washed him all over and even with the plant medicine some of the swelling from the ant bites had gone down some. It had been six hours since we had got back and with the boiling of the plants it was clear he looked much better. Solie placed different plants all over Peso's body and tried to get him to drink some of the broth from the plants and some water.

Then she opened his mouth and looked at where his tongue had been. I saw her search all through the plants and picked one odd looking plant that looked hard to the touch, with hair looking spears all over then she boiled some fresh water with this plant in it. She then cut up the now soft plant into thin layers, which reminded me of leaves. She then placed the plant over the place where they cut his tongue out, then closed his mouth. As I sit there watching, Foster came over and sat down beside me and watched for a while.

"Remind you'se of anyone. That looks like Red Bird when the bear attacked you'se and when she took care of Lizzie and Carolyn for all those months. Indian women don't know how to give up on people they love. Buck the horses need grass and the water is getting low. We'se need to be leaving this place."

"I think I can fine that green valley again. I'll ask Solie and we'll take all the horses and bring more water and cut some grass for the horses and tie it to Josephine's back. I want to see how Peso fairs. We'll leave BJ here to protect them."

I went and sat down close to where Solie was and watched the care she was taking with Peso. She looked at me with those dark eyes.

"Solie, we are low on water and the horses need grass. I can fine that valley where the water and grass is. Foster and me will leave in the morning and take all the horses. I'll leave all the water and food here so you can eat and take care of Peso and BJ with stay he is good with that gun and rifle and anyone has to watch for that bullwhip at his side."

"Why you do all this for?"

"I think all people need help sometime and I want to help. You remind me of my wife back home in Colorado Red Bird."

"She Indian?"

"Yes, her father is Chief Dancing Bear and we have four children."

"You happy to have so many little ones."

"Yes, very happy."

"You go to place and get water and grass. Be careful bad Indians came back all time. Try not leave tracks to follow."

In the morning we left and went straight there and saw no one. I had a hard time finding the place to go through to get into the valley but once in we found the water source. The evening before we left camp Solie had found time to search out five big gourds and hollowed them out to hold water. These we filled and the horses ate and we cut some grass from near the base of the boulders so it would be less noticeable to anyone that came along. Within two hours we started back and taking different paths with each horse would within a few hours leave little evidence of anyone being there. The grass we packed nice and tight and tied it to the back of Josephine, Foster's mule.

That evening just before the brilliant sun went down we were back in camp to find Peso sitting up drinking some broth. He still looked bad but the swelling was all gone and the ant bites were healing. I could still see the pain in his eyes but he was a strong brave and tried not to show any expression at all.

Foster cooked supper and I took some to Solie. Foster said that she hadn't touched the supply of food. I took a plate of food and some water.

"You need to eat Solie you will get sick and can't take care of Peso any longer."

"Me no eat till Peso can. It is my way."

"I didn't take Peso off that anthill so his woman can die. Look at him he is strong now. You have not eaten since you came to our camp and found Peso almost dead."

"Is true but have long way to go to be the same as before. Me wait to eat."

Peso looked at her with gentle but firm eyes and made some sign at her. Then she answered.

"Will eat when you up and strong."

Then he signed again.

"What is he saying?"

"I should eat, he says he will be all right and for me not to worry."

"He's right. Then what else was said?"

"Asked if you tell truth if you saved him from ants and sun. Told him covered with ants you cut him from ants and he could not believe a white man would do this for an Indian that not know."

I looked at Peso and said.

"Peso we need some help to fine where your people live and who is selling them rifles. I'll tell you the truth cause I know you will know if I lie. We were sent by the army to find this out so they can put an end to the killing of my people over the border. My son is with me to learn cause his grandfather, Dancing Bear, would think it was time to learn his way as a man should."

He made signs to Solie and then he turned on his side and closed his eyes.

"What did he say? Who did this to him? He must know."

"Say, will think about what you say in his sleep. He will tell you about what happened if he wants. It will be hard to do what you ask and only he can tell what happened. Let him rest and get stronger. Will eat now, know he will live."

She took the plate of food and a cup of water and looked at me in the eyes.

"Thank you, Buck Taylor."

The days went by slowly and Peso rested most of the time. After a week Peso was up and around for a few hours but his strength still was weak. His ant bites were now gone leaving some scars but he saw them as scars of battle to be proud of and the blisters from the sun was healed leaving his skin darker than ever. The worst was his tongue, which healed enough where he could eat slowly and with caution. During this time Solie taught me some sign so I could ask Peso questions myself. Foster watched and the sign he had forgotten started to come back. Foster had learned it from Dancing Bear when he and my great-grand father Jeb had come into the Colorado country. They had taught Dancing Bear English and when Dancing Bear learned enough they no longer talked with sign.

Another week passed and Peso was up all day making a bow with arrows and he went hunting and would bring back rabbits to cook. Now he had to always talk in sign.

"Me hunt for you. Saw you low on food and this cause of me. You have made many trips to get water and take care of our horses as you do yours. My way of showing me grateful."

Peso rode out on his horse one day and told Solie to stay with us till he returned.

"I will return with more meat."

I went up to him with a rifle and shells in my hand and held the rifle out to him.

"I know you use bow to hunt and make little noise but if you get in any danger use this. I give you as present from Foster and me. I have another."

He looked at me straight in the eyes and took the rifle out of my hands. For the eyes told of the truth deep in a man and this couldn't be changed. Then he jump on his horse and was gone without any words. I knew he was very grateful for this showed I trusted him fully. After he left Foster told me out of hearing of Solie.

"You'se think that was wise, Buck? We'se came here to try to get the guns from the Mescalero's not arm them."

"I think so. Now he knows we are friends and trust him. He is thought to be dead by his people at their hands I just bet you if not by them they would have gone back to their village by now and Solie said she is an outcast."

It was a few hours later and we saw a cloud of dust coming from the south fast. As it came closer we could see it was Peso with a mule deer across his horse but he rode straight pass us to the fire and jumped off and the deer fell hitting the ground hard but he seemed not to care as he threw dirt over the fire to put it out. He signed.

"Saw hunting party from our village. Saw me and chased me were yelling and know they would have killed me if caught. I do not know if still come my horse fast. Hope think I ghost." He laughed for the first time.

"Us hide with horses in rocks. Maybe not come. If find camp know I not dead. Would be trouble for us."

We rushed all our horses and bundles far up in the boulders with a good view all around. Not a dust cloud could be seen for miles around but we waited. The sun was near the western horizon when we decided to head back to camp.

"Peso, they must have thought you a ghost and maybe your horse to."

"Think so. Afraid to follow tracks may lead them to bad place they would not like."

Foster and me laughed as we ate the food Solie had fixed as a smile came across his face and then he became serious and the smile went the way of his tongue, gone.

"Maybe they think you were an evil spirit on the devil's horse." BJ put in. That brought another smile to Peso lips.

"Me, Solie have no people. Our people did this to us. I want to make peace with white man. To many come we never win. I want my people to live in peace. Not want to listen to me anymore so Victorio ordered this done. We can never go back but I still want to find a way for my people to live in peace. This is why I will help you and your people. Solie will come she my woman. I trust what you say. Solie tell me your woman is from a different tribe but Indian. You understand some of our ways."

"My wife, Red Bird comes from a man like you. He left his tribe with some others that felt like him. They made him Chief and have lived in the mountains where the sunsets not far from a town named Durango. The white people from town know Dancing Bear is their friend and never bother his people. Foster has known Red Bird since she was born. Maybe one day you will do the same. Some white men are not good just like some of your people are not good but maybe someday the good from both of our people can work together and both live in peace."

"This what I will pray to our God for."

We took a week to pack everything and Solie made Peso clothes from the tanned hide of the mule deer then she helped get the camp back to look like nature as best we could and Foster and Peso were great at this. Peso was to lead us across this desert and I would learn everything Peso knew about the beautiful but dangerous place called the desert that he would share with me. Foster and me sat and talked the night before we were to leave on the journey that would lead home one day. Peso and

Solie stayed to themselves this night. Since Peso had made up his mind to help us I had never heard a bad word from Solie about his decision.

3

The morning came in a flash then we were on the trail in behind Peso. We now had five people and five horses with a mule. There was no way to hide our trail so Peso didn't even try. The days were still hot but we had made our last run for water the day before. We went through lands that I never would imagine existed in this region not that far from Durango. The bright purple sage that looked so beautiful and the aroma of the sage would always be in my memory never to be forgotten. The sunsets and sunrises would have to be seen by each person and their mind would bring the beautiful hues of the different colors back from each person's memory to be relived over and over throughout one's life. I could see now that a good life could be lived in this region as long as one knew where the water was and there were some places that supported wildlife to be hunted for food. Each waterhole Peso lead us was well hidden out of sight of the normal eyes. Some were places that one just had to move a rock and water would come forth. Then there were the places that lead us into canyons that looked from a distance not to have any way out but the one we came in. Then it turned around a sharp corner or through a narrow passage that went into green pastures with abundance grass for our animals and game for our stomachs. This night was in that canyon where we made camp. As we were eating around the small campfire Peso signed and had Solie tell us.

"Here is where came as a boy. No one knows this place not even Solie. When go out of village on my trek to be warrior came to this place for a week. Father never knew I come here and not live in desert. Look deer for food plenty water to live and many plants for to eat or make well. Glad show Solie plants make well or I not be here, be in ground."

Foster and me laughed.

"That is true. We are glad to or we wouldn't have a new friend. My great grandfather had a place also that no one knew about and was killed but he hid a map to that place and Foster and me found his place that is rich with silver."

"Peso, back home we'se call him Silver Buck and he is known far and wide as a good man that will help any man in trouble but will hunt down any man that does wrong."

"Is good to hear about you and you about me. I think we will be good friends when this over. BJ are you good with whip."

"Go ahead BJ show them how good you are with your whip."

BJ unrolled his whip and in five fast flicks the cactus had five less red apples on top and not a crease in its body. A smile came across the mouths of both Peso and Solie.

Peso signed. "Could be handy someday."

That night it was very cool and the sounds of the coyotes sooth me as I slept. By sunrise we were on the trail again with fresh meat that Peso had killed and skinned out by sunrise. The breakfast that Solie had cooked was so delicious from what either Foster or me could make. We were so glad when Solie came to us and said "Peso no like you cook. I will cook this is my duty as woman."

BJ said. "Amend Solie, you're cooking is like my ma's."

"Good boy, you and wife have." She knew where to fine the things that were needed to bring out the favor of every piece of food we ate.

There were high buttes along the trail that rose out of the ground and reached up for the sky. These Peso rode up on to keep a lookout on our back trail and where he was leading us. The army couldn't come into Mexico but if they did they would soon be lost for some of these places that Peso took us through were like mazes that seemed to have no end. Some mornings I was so turned around that I thought we were going the way we came in the day before but Peso would only laugh and keep going.

Then one day at one in the afternoon Peso stopped and signed.

"Stop now wait till dark then show where village. Miles over ridge need to make sure where guards are by night. Solie no fire, eat dry meat. Give horses rest. Water, grass not far toward rising sun."

We staked the horses out after relieving them of their burdens. Then Solie filled all the water bags from the underground stream and brought the jerky for us to eat. We sat under the tree that was near the water. The wind was hot coming at us down the canyon but with the sweat on our bodies it felt like a cool breeze. Then right after the sun had gone down pass the mountains Peso came to us and he made sign to me.

"Solie rest will rise later and load the mule. Get ready to leave fast we walk now. No need her to sign, you learn my sign and we have to move fast. Foster old can move fast?"

"Yes, he is good on his feet. We come from place with giant mountains. I've seen him on a ledge two feet wide and two hundred feet in the air and not miss a step."

I turned to Foster and told him what Peso said.

"Why you'se whippersnapper I'se was fast as you before you was born. Now lead on I'se keep up."

"Like Foster, my friend. No harm meant." I told Foster and he turned red and ate his words.

"Peso my friend also. Even friends misunderstand each other sometimes."

"BJ keep whip close may need to use on guards and tie up with rope. Do not want to kill, some my friends not all want to do this to me."

Peso led the way into the dark of night. There was no moon this night that was good for us. He signed.

"Know where guards be. Need to make sure. Stay here, come back."

I had to get close to see his sign in the near pitch-black night.

He went out around a curve on the small butte and disappeared and came back in a few minutes.

"Around there can see all village when sun comes up in sky. Stay here till then. Guard not there."

"Will they see us in daylight?"

"Not if careful. Be back before sunrise, go to village see son try to get him come."

"Is that wise, may be seen."

"Not seen know how to get in and out. Say need some people to start own village to make peace and live by white man."

"I trust you to know what to do."

Peso was gone and we sit back to wait. From this height we would have a spectacular view of all the surrounding area.

****

Peso came to his son's teepee and made a small slit in the hide. It was dark with everyone fast asleep. He had to be careful cause Juan slept right next to Victorio teepee. Victorio has told Peso not to worry about his young son that he would become his father and train him in the art of war. Juan was only twelve in white man's years and was just starting his warrior training. Peso slipped to Juan's mat and just looked at him for a minute wishing he knew what would be in his son's mind when he saw his father alive and never to hear his voice again. He was taught how to talk with his hands at an early age.

Now he lightly put his big, scared hand over Juan's mouth and he instantly woke up but could not see who it was and tried to yell but Peso held his hand over his son's mouth tight and bend close to his face. When Juan's eyes adjusted to the dark he saw it was his father and stopped struggling and had a frighten look on his face. Peso started to sign after seeing that the boy was to frighten to yell.

"Do not be afraid son. I am your father and am much alive and have come to take you away from my enemy's they are no longer my people. They cut out my tongue so I can never speak the truth to our people. Must use sign to be heard. They tied me to anthill like an enemy but two good white men cut me loose when I was almost dead. Then your mother came and made me well after long time so that why not come for you till now. Must come to help start new village close to white man and learn his ways but never forget our ways. White men are too many for us to conquer. We will live in peace beside them." Juan spoke very low to his father.

"They say you die by white man's hands and I should hate them and kill them always but I have remembered what you say that we have to change and live in peace. This was hard to keep in my mind knowing that I would never see you or my mother again. I will come now I know they were lying to me for I see you with the scars they put on you for everyone to see."

"We must take a pony for you to ride and gather your knife and I see they gave you a rifle and bring your blanket to sleep. Must hurry before sun rises in the sky. Friends wait on butte."

Peso tied skins over the pony's hoofs so no noise would be heard. He led his son out of the village forever and into a new life. The butte came to them fast in the dark soon to be dusk. At the top Silver Buck and Foster were watching as they came to the top into camp.

******

"Buck, my son Juan. He speaks your tongue. Will learn your way fast as I will and his mother will. Juan this is our other friends Foster and BJ son of Buck you learn from him all you can. My hope will be you make good friends."

I extended my hand and Juan took a step back and looked in his father's eyes.

"This the white man way of saying good friend."

Peso took Bucks hand and shook it and then Foster's and BJ's hand and so Juan did the same and saw the three new white men smile at him. This was to be his first lesson in the white man's way and he would always remember this first contact all his life. Then Foster spoke to Juan.

"Juan, just call him Silver all his friends do."

"Now Foster you didn't have to bring that up. I see you got away with a horse that will come in handy if we have to get away fast."

"Solie will be ready when get back will go fast out of enemies country."

The sun was up now and the village was in plain sight as I made a mental note and we left on the trail we came up. The village was still quiet as we went out of sight. Solie had some food ready and we ate fast and saddled our horses as Juan went to his mother and they both had tears in their eyes.

We were up on our horses and heading to the border with Arizona. We could move fast now that we had Peso with us for he knew where the water was but we were running low on food and there weren't any nearby towns. Peso went out with Juan to hunt so we had plenty of meat. Solie picked berries and other plants to make the meal better but Foster and me needed sugar and coffee and some spices to make a meal with some eggs and flour for breakfast.

"We need to get some things in a town to make a good breakfast. We'll show Solie how to make eggs with the meat and pancakes for Juan. He will love them with maple syrup as BJ does."

"You can bet on that." BJ said smiling.

"No town for long ways north. Only been near once. Is near where white men live with Indians and Mexicans sell Mescalero's rifles and other things that women like, live many miles. Take seven suns to be there."

"We need to know where these white men live. The army is looking for these men to stop them. We call them Comancheros and they are evil. They sell Indians whiskey that makes them act crazy."

"Is true, have seen with my eyes. Those white men are so bad even Indians kept distant except when need rifles or bullets. Will show way to big town with white man."

The nights were as cold as the days were hot and this night was no exception. With the sky clear the stars shining as bright as diamonds far as the eyes could see and the howl of the desert coyote was as sweet as a lullaby to put one to sleep and this night the moon stayed hidden from my sight as my eyes closed and didn't reopen till the dawn was coming up from the eastern sky. Solie had a good breakfast cooking over the fire and Peso and Juan had the horses ready for the trail. Foster had loaded the supplies onto Josephine and only had to wait till we ate for the cooking pans and we would be gone deeper into the desert. Peso sat down and made sign.

"Me no like, to peaceful. Me, Juan go back trail, watch maybe gone all day. Come if trouble. Know Victorio miss Juan by now. Had to see trail we left. Woman know way."

"You go, I was wondering about that myself. Seems Victorio would have big plans for Juan after taking him in and wouldn't like that he left in the dead of night."

Peso pointed out landmarks for us to follow as he and Juan went back on our back trail. We went north but by noon it seemed we were going on an incline and had to rest the horses more often. We now came to water that was flowing freely in the open and the vegetation was becoming thicker than before and by nightfall we were among some small pine trees. Solie made supper and then sit but wouldn't eat.

"What's wrong Solie? That was a mighty fine supper you'se fixed. You should eat." Foster said.

"Cannot, just think what Victorio do to Peso if catch him again. May not wait for ants to eat."

"I've been thinking about that and I know Peso will be careful this time and he'll think of something to throw them off our trail."

****

Peso and Juan were far behind where we parted. "Juan, climb up on cliff and see what coming."

Juan made his way up to the top of the cliff, like only a twelve-year-old could. He looked around and then Peso saw him hit the ground hard. He motioned that they were coming from the south and he hurried down.

"What are going to do? They are coming right up our trail."

"Do as I tell you."

Peso jumped down quick and rolled in the dirt built up on the side of the trail. The dirt was like fine power that covered him from head to toe. He was the color of red rock that lines some of the canyons.

"Now you take the rope and led me up the trail and stop right in front of them and tell them the story."

"What story?"

"You dug me up and put me on my horse. Know you think of more."

They rode on till they saw them coming and Juan stopped and looked sad. The ten braves just stopped a little ways off and kept looking at them.

"They not come closer."

"Then ride right up to them, see what happens."

So Juan led the horse with Peso on it even closer and the braves just looked and their horses were getting nervous, prancing around in circles but the eyes of the braves never left the sight of the coming. Juan stopped right in front of them.

"I want to talk to Victorio. I dug up my father where my mother buried him and I want to show Victorio that the marks on my father are not marks that white man make when kill Indian. They are marks of how Indian kill."

"Take him away Victorio not here send us brave warriors to find you and bring back to village."

"As you can see my father is still covered with his burial dirt but he is very much alive."

They laughed at him as he let go of the rope and Peso horse leaped forward pass Juan toward the braves and at the same time Peso threw up his arms toward the sky and tried to yelled the terrible Mescalero war cry. They couldn't get their horses turned around fast enough. They kept running into one other and as they galloped away over the cactus and the brush Juan yelled.

"Tell Victorio my father spirit will find him one day and get even."

"My son do fine job with those brave warriors. Give a few suns head start on them. Back to mother and our new friends."

As they hurried back Peso turned and signed. "This has been my home for all my many moons. With its deep canyons and high treeless mountains and secret places for water that only us and the animals know. Peso will miss it but will get use to our new home and you can tell your children about the dry desert you came from. Never let it leave heart and spirit for one day you may have to return."

They rode toward where the others would be heading, riding up straight and proud. That night they rode into camp.

****

"Where you get all covered with dirt?" BJ asked.

"Long story, Buck we have five or six sun lead ahead than before."

Paso went and poured water over him and Solie took a rag and rubbed him. Then brought him and Juan food.

The next day we headed out again toward Flagstaff. With the Indians off our trail for a while we had a little time to relax. The vegetation was getting greener and thicker and we were going up higher. We came to creeks and even some flowing streams now and again.

"Be in town two suns. You three go in we stay out. Men might know Paso from when buy rifles."

BJ never missed time at night away from the fire to practice with his bullwhip and Juan was always sitting watching then the night before we were going to town BJ put his whip in Juan's hands.

"You try and then I'll show you."

Juan took it and tried to make snap loud but could not make it do the loud noise. BJ wrapped his hand around Juan's wrist and pulled it back and then fast-forward and it came forth with the loud pop and a big smile came across Juan's face. BJ let go and Juan did it by his self.

"Your son is a fast learner."

"Yes, but your son is a better teacher."

"When BJ made that in me'se shop, I'se didn't think he would ever quit trying to crack that whip but he never gave up. Now it's a part of him like that six-gun is to you'se Silver."

"Now he's as fast with that whip as with that gun. They can both be deadly in his hands."

"Be careful town bad men test new men coming in to see what made of. Your eyes might pick the bad ones out and they will know where the leaders of the Comancheros are. If can show the bad ones up the others might not show it but will respect you more. May still kill but with respect."

"This man right here has more strength and skill with that gun than three men and more brains than ten of them."

"May need that and more before the sun goes down tomorrow."

"Thank you BJ for teaching my son your whip but in town be careful when use whip. Let it be a surprise how can use it. Do not let them know how good are till right time and Buck and Foster will know when that time comes."

4

The morning was downright cold since we came up that long slope off the desert floor. Solie had fixed a good breakfast for us and we were gone. The pine trees were getting taller and thicker as we moved further up the low range mountains. About noon we stopped by a stream, now there was water every mile or so, and ate while the horses grazed on the nice thick grass beside the stream. They had seemed to put back on their weight since the experience in the desert. The trail that we were on led to a wagon road that had to been made by men that wanted a wider trail to get needed things into town. As we gained the top of the upward slope there was the town like it just sprung up right there in front of us. It could be seen that a great many people had taken a lot of time to clear enough ground of trees for space for all the buildings that stood at the bottom of the slope we were now descending.

Then three riders rode up to us out of nowhere and stopped right in our path. I turned Blacky to the right and Foster and BJ went to the left around the men and kept a steady pace. One of the men yelled.

"Senor, do not you know what it means when three men stop right in your path?"

"I thought you might be in a big rush to get to the saloon as we are to get to the general store to buy badly need supplies." I said as I looked back as we moved on. The man that spoke rode up beside me, the other two were on the other side of BJ and Foster. He had a big smile on his face as he spoke again.

"That is good for you to spend you pesos in this town. But it is my job to make sure who is coming into Senor Martin's town. He might skin us alive if not we find out your name and your business here. Now I know your business, to buy supplies, but I still do not have the names of you three. My name is Tope and these two are Louise and Beets, see how red he turns when his name is spoken, but his hand is quick. Now it would be nice to know your names before Senor Martin find us talking in the middle of the road and I did not find out your names."

"Does Mr. Martin really own all this town and the land around?" I stopped Blacky in the middle of the road and made a sweeping swing of my arm around the whole area. "He must be very rich man to own so much."

"I am starting to become very impatience with you. Your name please right now."

I looked him straight in the eyes.

"Well, why didn't you say what you wanted much more clearer? I'm Buck and this here lad is my son BJ and this is my old grandpa Foster."

Foster looked at me with a blank stare and just turned up his nose in the air like he smelled a skunk.

"Now that was very kind of you, now get your supplies and get out of town, pronto, understand?"

"I see you have a very nice-looking hotel down this long street. We have been on the trail many weeks and were thinking of taking a room and getting a bath and a nice home cooked meal."

"I am sorry but I am just a low peon and that decision must be left up to Senor Martin. Now I need a last name, if you please and then you can buy your supplies and I will see what Senor Martin says about you staying."

"Why, Taylor is our name."

He turned and pointed to the general store.

Be our guess and I'll be back with Senor Martin's decision."

We headed on down the slope onto the main street of Flagstaff, Arizona. At the end of the main street was a mountain that rose a good five hundred feet that left most of the street in the shadow till noon or later. Also at the end of main was the blacksmith with the stable and corral. They were backed up against the bottom of the tree-lined mountain. This is when BJ interrupted my thoughts.

"What will we do now?"

"Wait and see what Martin says. We still have had a good look at the town and the people in it. It seems this Martin is the boss around here so he is probably the head of the Comancheros. Don't mention that around any of these town folks."

"Silver, what's that talk about me'se being a grandpa."

"Well Foster, you sure look like a grandpa. Just play the part. Anyway you are like the children's three grandpa anyway."

"Never thought of it that way. I'se kind of like that."

We tied up in front of the general store and stepped up on a nice porch with an overhang that covered the whole porch with a wood walkway that went in both directions from the store. There were three saloons, this general store, and the livery at the end of the street then two diners that looked like they stayed busy, as did the saloons. I noticed that no sheriffs' office was anywhere to be seen. But there was a dressmaker shop with hats in the window. We stepped in the cool interior of the general store and it was about the same as most other general stores in most other towns except I saw no guns or rifles and no ammunition behind the counter. That was very strange in this kind of country where hunting for your meat was common. We looked around the store since the clerk was busy with others. As I looked around all the men were not carrying guns on their hips but a very few and they were rough looking. This made me think that these men with the guns were part of the gang of Comancheros and the ones without were regular town people.

"Foster, you noticed there are no guns or ammunition in this store."

"I'se notice that."

BJ had his bullwhip wrapped around his shoulder up under his arm pit like a coil of rope with the strong wood handle hanging down by his side, where his .45 hung at his hip ready to be grabbed and used on a seconds notice. That's when the man behind the counter came over.

"May I help you with anything in particular. I have most everything that a man could want. My name is Simon and I run this store for Mr. Martin."

"Here's my list that we will be needing for the trail."

He looked at the list and then looked back at me.

"I have everything except the ammunition that is handled by Mr. Martin and his men."

"Why's that?"

"I guess just a precaution against the wrong people having it."

"And what kind of people would that be?"

"I have no idea but you can discuss that with Mr. Martin's man Tope. That's him coming in the front door. I'll get everything else on your list ready."

Sure enough Tope walked right up to us with that big smile on his ugly face. Looking around him I could see Louise and Beets standing outside the front door one on each side with cigarette hanging from each ones mouth.

"Senor Taylor, it is good to see you again. I see you are getting your supplies. This is good. I have more good news Senor Martin has agreed for you and your party to stay at the hotel one night with your horses to be stabled at the livery. Let me warn you, you must stay in your room except to eat a meal at the diner and if you like one drink at one of our outstanding saloons."

"Why is it to be that way?"

"That is what Senor Martin wants. He wants this town to be very peaceable at all times or you could mount up and spend the night on the trail many miles away for Senor Martin's lands stretch over many miles."

"Then that will do. But we do need some ammunition for the trail. You know for hunting for food and protection. You know we have no one like Senor Martin to protect us out in the wilderness."

"That can be arranged when you leave town in the morning. I will have some forty five's ready. I happened to notice you have 44-40's on your saddles. I'll have some of those also. I hope you enjoy you bath and your night in our grand hotel."

"I'm sure we will and we can eat breakfast in the morning before we leave."

"Why of course. It is our pleasure. So have a great night. Adios amigo."

"Adios."

"This is a strange town." Foster said to us.

"Yea Pa, that one is just too nice to suit me."

"I'm sure that's why he's got the job of greeting new people that come into town. But I'm sure if you cross him he can be meaner than he is nice."

"You have that right."

We turned and Simon had just said that.

"What else can you tell us?"

"Nothing, I said to much. Just be careful tonight not to leave your room after you eat cause you will have someone watching your doors every minute of the night. Here's your order."

Simon looked around,

"Anything you don't want anyone looking at take with you to your room and your rifles."

"You saying they will go through our things."

"Anything really important take with you when you go to eat."

"They'll go through our rooms?"

Beets walked in the store with his rifle in the crook of his arm and looked at us.

"Good to have your business Mr. Taylor hope you and your son and father enjoy your night in town. Good-by."

We picked up our three bundles and packed them on the mule and walked down the street to the livery. As we walked in the shadow of the barn BJ called out.

"Anyone here."

That's when an old man came into view.

"I may be old but I'm not deaf. No call to holler at me."

"Sorry mister, we didn't see anyone."

"That's all right young feller. We don't get many visitors in town so I'm usually out back with the horses that belong to Mr. Martin. He's very particular with those critters."

"We just want to stable our animals for one night with grain and hay and if you can a rub down. They've been on the trail a long while."

"Even that mule critter."

That's when Foster spoke up.

"Yes, even that mule old man. She's me'se pride and joy."

"Don't get riled up so much. Just asking and what you mean old man you're old enough to be my father."

"Silver, that did it. Can I'se hit him now."

"Foster that's it. I told you about calling me that in town."

"He just got me so riled up calling me old."

"You are Silver Buck, I heard of you up Colorado way."

"Kept that to yourself if you don't mind."

We turned and there in the doorway of the barn was Beets.

"I'll take good care of your animals even the rub down. That will be ten dollars for the extra rub down and oats." Then he leaned close to me and whispered as he pretended to drop the money I handed him.

"Don't worry Silver I'm not one of his men I just try to stay alive 'til they decided to leave Flagstaff."

"Thanks"

"Orin, the name. Orin Ward at your service."

I shook his hand. "I'm Buck Taylor and this is BJ my son and grandpa Foster."

We took our bundles and rifles with our saddlebags and headed to the hotel. As we passed Beets I said.

"Hello Beets." His face turned all red.

The hotel was just as most in the west. Large front porch with rockers lined up on each side of the double doors. Then the usual old timers sitting rocking or whittling ready to talk about most things that happen around town then one of the old timers spoke to BJ.

"Say, youngster that bullwhip that you have there around your shoulder do you know how to use it? I used to be pretty darn good with one."

"Sure do mister. Here would you like a try with mine."

BJ unwrapped the bullwhip and as the man raised out of his chair BJ handed it to him. He took it and said.

"Mighty fine weigh." He snapped it in the air a few times.

"Good snap and balance. See that can on the side of the sidewalk. Watch!"

He stepped off the porch and let the whip fly. That tin can jumped in the air and before it hit the ground he popped it again and again and it didn't touch the ground until he stopped.

"Well I'll be I still has something left in me. Sonny, you think you can out do's that?"

The old timer handed the bullwhip back to BJ and he wound it around his shoulder.

"Well sir, you're all mighty good. Tell you the truth I'm still working at getting that good but I know it will take a while."

"You just keep practicing and you'll get better. Good to meet another whipper like me. My name's Bill Masters, I've been around these parts many a years."

BJ grabbed Bill's hand, smiled and shook it hard.

"My name's BJ Taylor and it's good to meet someone I can try to match someday."

"Glad to get a chance to show you how it's done."

As we walked into the hotel the other men in the rocking chair were patting Bill on the back and we heard them say.

"You sure showed that youngster a thing or two."

The desk clerk looked at us through his thick horn-rimmed glasses. Looked like he was astonished that we were there.

"You are new. When did you go to work for Mr. Martin?"

"We don't work for him and we don't plan to."

"No one stays here that don't have permission from him."

The door opened and Beets stuck in his head.

"It's all right Senor Ben, Mr. Martin said it was OK."

"Why didn't someone let me know?"

"Senor Ben, that is what I think I just did."

"I'm sorry boys but Martin's men are sometimes lacking." He pointed with his head.

"Could we have two rooms?"

"Sure thing. Don't get many guess that don't work for Martin. Glad to have someone from the outside."

"Could we have the two rooms across from each other?"
"Sure thing."
He handed us the keys and I gave one to Foster as we went up the stairs.
"What's the idea's Buck?"
"I'll tell you in the room. Come on in our back room."
We all went in and unloaded all our packs.
"Foster, I may have to go out tonight to find out some things. They will most likely be watching this back room. They won't expect you to be trying to get around in the dark. I'll come through your room and go out over the front rail. Now let's go eat. I'm sure they will go through our things so I'm taking these paper with me."

When we got to the diner the place was packed and most looked to work for Martín with their low hanging guns on their hips. All eyes turned to us as we sit down at our table. The waiter came over to take our orders and brought our coffee. As we sat there and men started to leave two of them came up to our table and stared down at us. I looked up and asked in a cool, calm voice.

"May I help you two with something."

"No, just looking at three people I would do anything to get my hands on but Senor Martin said you were to be left alone. So be it." They walked out the door taking with him his scared-up face and the other vaquero just as ugly. About then another vaquero came by and stopped at our table.

"I sure hope you go out of your room tonight and I'm the one that gets to put a bullet in your heart."

"I tell you if I go out I'll look you up." About then our supper showed up and we ate in peace. As we finished we got up and I turned to the crowd of men.

"It sure was nice eating with a bunch of nice cowboys like you with great conversation. Goodnight. By the way we will be in the saloon for one short drink."

As we got outside Foster turned to look at me. I smiled cause I knew he wanted more.

"Sure thing Foster have two or three you'll sleep better and I'll have a first beer with my son."

"You mean it Pa?"

"Sure son. Just one beer, that's all I ever have."

We walked into the Lazy Chance Saloon and walked up to the bar to order two beers and three whiskeys. As we paid and took them to the table again all eyes were on us as we sat and slowly drank our drinks. As we got up to leave I turned once again.

"Since you'll probably be up all night take a good look at me so you'll know what I look like if you lay an eye on me in the dark night. But all for nothing cause I'll be snoring away in my front room at the hotel."

They were all grumbling as we went out on the street and headed to the hotel. Now all we needed was to wait 'til dark and Foster to fall asleep like a log.

"Good night Foster get a good night sleep we'll leave early in the morning."

"I'se going out with you tonight."

"No just me. You sleep well."

As I thought, they had gone through everything and left a mess not caring if we knew. I told BJ to lie down and rest for he was going out with me tonight.

"Me!"

"Yes, someone has to cover my back but we have to be quiet and be very careful."

As I laid in bed watching the sun set in the west behind the giant pine trees it took me back when I first got to Colorado and all the men that were trying to get Jeb's silver mine and then my eyes were shut and the next thing I knew BJ was shaking me awake.

"Pa it's been dark for two hours. I can hear Foster snoring."

"Bring you .45 and bullwhip. Might come in handy. If you have to use it make it count cause they will know who was there. Here, let's make our beds look like we're sleeping."

We put one of our bundles in each bed and brought the sheet up over the pillows. I looked out our window and there was Tope and Louise down at each end of the ally. As I turned the knob slowly, not to make any noise, and cracked open the door then looked down the hall both ways there was Beets in a chair leaning against the wall with his hat over his eyes. He had to be asleep so we went to Foster's room and went inside. As BJ came in I saw him look toward Beets.

"Still asleep." He whispered and so was Foster as we crossed to the window and looked out. I could hear music and loud talking coming from each saloon but that was half way down the street. Lucky the moon wasn't out yet it was pitch black.

"BJ just follow me and keep an eye in all direction as I will be. I don't know what we're looking for but I think I'll know if we see it."

Out the window we went and over the railing then we dropped to the ground and got our backs flat against the wall in the shadows. We made our way out a ways from the light of the town. Then we worked our way through the trees and then saw a dim light up the slope from where we were.

"BJ, look up there, that must be where Martin lives it overlooks the town."

It wasn't much of an uphill walk but as we made our way up we ran right into some kind of building. Then BJ tripped over something in front of this large building and as he got up BJ got my attention.

"Pa, some kind of metal." I went back and looked and there were metal tracks and they led to this building, which was a railcar. We worked our way up and there were two rail cars and then we came to the steam engine. As I looked on up there were three more men with rifles coming from the house toward the train. We turned and went down the slope and there we saw the rail tracks were covered up with pine needles, which were all around thick as thieves. The three men were closer so we hid under the last rail car behind the wheels. They stopped right in front of where we were and were rolling a smoke and talking.

"When is the next shipment of rifles due?"

"This train will leave tomorrow after we see those three get out of the area. It should be back from Santa Fe in a week or so. Those three sure delayed the start but the barn is full and have enough for Chief San Juan which is going to be here before then and Victorio will be here by the time the train gets back."

"Mr. Martin sure has a set up here. No one in town will get out of hand as long as they have no one to lead them."

"That's why those three have to be rushed out of town. That one looks to be a leader and the boss says he thinks he's heard that name somewhere but can't remember where."

The three scattered into the night of total darkness. I whispered to BJ.

"We have to get a look at that Martin. He thinks he's heard of me might be someone I know from the past before you were born. Let's go son slow up to the house and we'll head back and wake Foster and get out of this town."

We worked our way pass the railcars and engine. Then there were pine trees to hide behind all the way to the house. I could see that the moon was coming up over the horizon and bright as ever. We had our backs against the side of the house where a light was shining.

"BJ, bend over I need to get up on your back to see in the window."

I climbed on his back and had a look inside and got one of the biggest surprises of my life. A man was talking to a woman and had his back to me and they were laughing and as the man took a drink from the glass he was holding in his hand he turned and just for a second I saw his full face and it was as if I was transported back twenty years. I lost my balance and tumbled to the ground. As I got up I heard the man inside run to the window and look out.

"We have to get out of here fast follow me."

The man was yelling out orders and men were rushing to the house and we were off down the slope and then the barn came in sight and I knew no matter the danger I had to see how many rifles were in there. We went to the back where I saw the door to the hayloft was open.

"Pa, we have to get out of here."

"Just one minute bend over again I need your back. I could barely reach the ledge of the open loft but I managed to pull myself up inside the loft. There on the barn floor below was two guards with lanterns looking through the barn and there were the rifles a quick guess was about twenty cases and the men left the barn and I was over the edge and dropped to the ground and we were off through the piney woods down the slope when a man was right in front of us. The man from the diner that wanted to put a bullet in my heart. He had a big smile on his face.

"I won't yell for help you're all mine."

A shot would bring all the men straight to us but before I could react I heard BJ's bullwhip fly through the air and catch the gun out of the man's hand and then another lash went around the man neck that brought him to the ground and he was out cold. I grabbed his belt and tied his hands and put his handkerchief in his mouth and we were down the slope and into the main street of town. There were men coming down a long ways behind us. The hotel was right in front of us and we ran right in the front door and made the stairs three steps at a time. At the top was Beets waking up and pulling his gun and mine came out and went off and Beets wouldn't turn red anymore.

"Get Foster and I'll get our things."

Foster opened the door as BJ reached for the doorknob.

"Foster, grab your things BJ will help you they're on our tail."

We went down the back steps and there in our way was Tope and Louise with guns drawn. BJ had his whip cracking in the air as my .45 came out his whip caught Tope's gun and my slug went through Louise's hand and he dropped his gun.

We tied them up fast and headed for the livery. As we got closer to the back of the livery I couldn't believe my eyes there were our horses in the back already to go.

"I heard the commotion and just knew it had to be you. Good luck and come back and help us if you can." Orin said. I turned and said.

"I'll be back." As we left down the ally and out of town by now the men were on their mounds and trying to find our trail but in the dark they would have a hard time. We headed for camp where we had left Peso, Solie and Juan but when we reached the camp just before dawn they were not there and no sign of a camp having been there. Then I heard a sound behind me. We turned and saw Juan.

"Move camp know might have trouble." Juan got off his pony and tied large pieces of brush behind each of our horses as I saw was behind his pony and he jumped on his bareback pony and left and we followed. We looked at the trail down and I said.

"Juan is that loose slate going down."

"First part bad with slate, as you call it very loose. Is why not many men go down this way? The other way takes days more."

"Blacky and Lagger have dealt with this but BJ's horse Red hasn't so BJ, you come down last and follow as close to our trail as you can. This slate can slide out from under the horses hoof and Red will be frighten and not know what to do so just pat him to reassure him and kept him calm as we go down. Go slow Juan, you are used to this we are not."

We started down and Juan's pony took to it like it was a trail through the forest but at first even Blacky and Lagger were having a slow time but Josephine, Foster mule was taking it great. The slate was sliding under the horse's hoofs so as I looked back I could see that Red was really nervous but BJ was talking to him as he patted him on the neck as they moved down the canyon trail. Around the fourth bend in the trail a rattlesnake came out of the underbrush in front of Blacky and he reared up on his hind leg with a loud whiney that reverberated through the canyon and came down hard on the rattler that smacked in the head of the snake but this caused Red to rear up but BJ handled him and he only slide a few feet and regained his footing as we continued down the canyon wall. The slate ended and we found we could move along much faster.

It was dawn by the time we reached the new camp that was down in a deep canyon thick with vegetation beside a fast-running river maybe a hundred feet across at this point. As we had been coming down the long trail, maybe a mile or more of winding trails, with a drop off on one side and a wall of rock that went straight up where we had been on the other.

We had looked out over a canyon to beat all canyon's the beauty of it was untellable it had to be seen by oneself and it looked never ending. It was the grandest canyon ever to be seen by man and I would have never known that our new camp was down here. There was no way it could be seen from above. This sight would be in my mind 'til my death.

"Good to see you three. Hope get back soon. Move camp, to open where was. Here are hidden. Stay as long as need to. No one knows trail down here except Indians and do not come this way much is hard, very hard to follow trail down. Now you eat Solie fix you eat." Peso signed.

"It's good to see you. This is a fine camp and well hidden. Now we eat and I'll tell you what happen. Peso what is this river called?"

"White man call it Colorado but we call it "River of many Colors" and some tribes call "Thunder River" hear the roar."

I told Peso what when on in town and the people were under the guns of real corrupt men. Then I added.

"There is a barn with hundreds of rifles for Chief San Juan, he'll be there in a few days and a train that will bring more rifles for Chief Victorio in a week from Santa Fe. I need to find a way to destroy the rifles and get rid of that evil man Walters again."

Foster's head came up and he stopped eating.

"Why you'se say that Silver. You'se know they hung Walters for having Jeb killed."

"I know, I killed his son but when I got on BJ's back to look into the house to see what this Martin looked like, I swear there before me was the face of Walters and no other. I just don't know it was the spitting image of Walters and the woman with him was different but looked like Jenny Walters."

"You'se know she died for sure we buried her at the bottom of that cliff."

"I know, it has to be some kin of theirs using the name of Martin. But whoever we have to stop them."

"You'se were to report what we found to General Cook and we'se would be done."

"I know but in five days to a week hundreds if not a thousand rifles will be in most of the Mescalero bands hands to raid and kill. We have to try to stop that from happening."

"We'se didn't even get more shells for our guns. How will we'se stop them?"

This is when Peso started to sign fast.

"Slow down Peso I can only understand slowly."

He slowed down. "Is a man named Williams half days ride from here to south. Has trading post. Seen guns and bullets in his store. Would not sell to Peso cause Indian. Saw many times sell to white men. Saw a room far from back of store. Said what says sign. He made a big boom with his mouth and his hands were together and came up and wide apart like a big cloud. Said for white miners and rancher to get rid of tree stumps and boulders."

"Dynamite, Foster that's it. Thank you Peso can you led us to this Williams trading post."

"That's what, Silver."

"We blow up the barn and the train with all the rifles. Then General Cook can bring in the army and round-up everyone."

"Sounds good but that train leaves for Santa Fe tomorrow morning."

"We have to leave right after we eat."

"Peso led, Juan stay here take care of mother and camp."

We left up the trail to the top of the canyon, which was the slowest part of the trip but it was faster than coming down and the next time down should be easier for the horses. As we were riding through the large and small pine trees I rode up beside Peso. He signed. "Watch for Victorio may be looking for Juan and see me, be in big trouble."

"The men from Flagstaff may be out looking for us."

We kept out of sight as much as possible. By noon we were within sight of the trading post but stopped as three horses were tied up to the hitching rail. We sat and watched for a while.

"Son, you and me are the only ones that can take care of those three if they are Martin's men. Foster, you and Peso stay here with Josephine.

You'll know when to come in. Peso if you hear shooting then you know these are the bad men from Flagstaff. If one gets away you stop him. I am sure you are a good shot from all of the meat you provided our camp. Son, can you do this with your pa."

"Yes, Pa I saw what they have done to a good town and its people."

"Peso wants to be friends with white man but they are bad to you will shoot to protect us."

We rode up to the post and saw eyes looking at us through the open door as the three stepped out on the wide porch of the store. There was the one called Pedro and two others I had not seen before. As we dismounted Pedro spoke up with that same big smile on his face as Tope.

"We have been looking for you senor. It was not nice what you did to Beets and Louise and then you tied me up as you did Tope. We have told Senor Williams to watch for you but now he does not have to. We will take you back for the murder of Beets and wounding of Louise."

"Did you tell Mr. Williams how Mr. Martin and his men have taken over the town and taken away all the guns from the good people."

"No, cause this is not true we only want to protect the people for their own good."

"How about selling rifles to the Mescalero's?"

"How could I tell him this when it is not true? Now come with us or we will have to shoot you down like the murderer you are."

"You can try but I'm sure that Mr. Williams has some shovels in his store to bury you up on that hill over there. I only tied you up cause, for some strange reason, I found I liked you and Tope. But now I don't know what that reason was."

"BJ, you take the one on the right and remember what grandpa taught you."

"This little boy is going to shoot Big Poncho."

BJ spoke up. "Big as you are I can't miss."

We saw Mr. Williams laugh and a smile came across Pedro's face.

"Mr. William stay in your store this won't take long. Then we can talk. We aren't going anywhere with you three so let's get on with it. Any time you're ready."

5

At that minute the three tried to draw but their guns were only just clearing leather when BJ's bullet caught Big Poncho right in the chest and he went flying back against the wall of the store. Then my bullets hit Pedro right between the eyes and he tumbled from the porch to the dusty trail and the other man caught my second shot right in the stomach and he dropped his gun in the dirt and held his stomach as he dropped to his knees and fell face first and rolled over yelling for someone to help him. As we rushed to him I saw Peso and Foster coming fast on the road to the store. Then I looked at the man as Mr. Williams came out of his trading post but it was too late the man had yelled his last time in the high country. Mr. Williams brought the shovels and we bury the three behind a huge boulder back of the post.

"Is what you said true is Martin selling rifles to the Mescalero's? What is this one doing with you? I've seen him before he tried to buy a rifle from me."

Peso signed. "For hunting food for my family."

"Why don't he talk?"

"Victorio had his tongue cut out cause he was talking about peace with the whites and had him staked out on an anthill. We found him and cut him loose and he nearly died from the ant bites and sun. He is trying to help us stop a bloody war. Here are papers from General Cook."

I handed him the papers and he read it and handed it back.

"Now we are in a hurry. We need shells for our guns and Peso said he heard you talk about dynamite for the ranchers and miners."

"Back in the shed and I have plenty of shells of all kinds help yourself. The dynamite, there is only three crates of it but you know it is very dangerous and you have to know about putting the fuses in the sticks of dynamite cause they have to ride separated."

Foster spoke up. "You'se just put them there fuses in my saddlebags and I'se take care of the rest. I'se was mining for gold and silver in Colorado before you'se were born."

"I'll say you sure look old enough."

"Why you'se young whippersnapper."

"Now Foster." We all laughed.

"Come in and we'll get everything together."

Mr. Williams left with BJ and Peso behind him and went up back through the knee-high grass. Each one was carrying a box and he left the door open.

"I'm expecting another shipment next week Henry will just have to wait this is much more important than any boulders or stumps."

"Pa, that's just an old outhouse."

"Yea, big enough for my needs and the dynamite I keep on hand."

"Isn't that kind of dangerous."

"Na, I kept the fuses right here."

He handed them to Foster. "Make sure the fuses are long enough. You don't want to blow yourself up."

"There, he'se goes again Silver."

"Foster, I told you about that."

"I'se sorry Buck."

"Why I'll be, you're the one from Colorado that found the huge silver mine and this is your grandpa's best friend. I read all about you fifteen years ago or more. You must had been this young man's age when you two found that mine."

"I was and now just forget that you heard that."

We loaded the dynamite on Josephine and fuses in the saddlebags and enough shells to arm a small army and we bought two sawed off shotguns with plenty of twelve-gauge shells for close up fighting. Fire just one of them and it can take out three or four men at once. Then we bought four more rifles and four .45 colts and more ammunition. I paid Mr. Williams and shook his hand and as we rode off toward Flagstaff he yelled. "Let me know how it turns out."

I turned around in my saddle with one hand on the cantle and the other with the reins then said. "You might can hear it from here."

I waved good-bye.

We headed down the trail to Flagstaff but when we get there I had to figure out what was going to be our next move. I knew what had to be done but how to get it done was the problem. This whole area was depending on what happened to those rifles. The only people that knew how much danger they were in were the people of Flagstaff that the Comancheros had taken control of. I knew some of the people I had met would help if they had weapons to fight with. That is why I bought extra weapons just in case they would help us. We didn't know how many men that Martin had but I do know we had gotten rid of five now that was a small start. As we went through the thick forest of pines and furs Foster stopped in the middle of the deer trail we were following.

"Buck, look at this. We'se are cutting a trail of many shod horses and look over there some unshod horses. They'se mixed together and they'se are wide apart. I'se just bet that some of Martin's men and Chief San Juan's braves are both looking for our trail."

Peso and me swung off our horse and Peso walked the tracks a ways and came back and signed.

"Are braves from Mescalero's. Trailing to find us. Take to the rocky ground. May still find, will take longer."

"Maybe the time we need to finish this job and then head toward the train coming from Santa Fe."

Peso took to the boulders and rocky trails up to the higher elevations that may mislead the bunch looking for us. By the time they found our trail it would be too dark to follow and we would be back in Flagstaff and with them out looking for us there would be a lot less men to deal with in town. For the next few days we would not get much sleep and the food would be our last resort jerky. Up this high the air became thinner and made you tire faster. The sky was clearer this high up except for a few clouds that floated pass us on our way to the east. Then Peso came to me and pointed about three miles down our back trail west of us. He signed.

"Found trail but dark soon sundown. White man will not go at night. You follow Peso and take to town before moon up. Braves might follow but fewer of them."

I turned back to BJ to see how he was and Foster.

"How you doing son and you Foster? We're going to keep on till we make Flagstaff and think I'll talk to Orin, Bill and Simon about helpin' us some."

"Pa, I'm so excited that I don't think I could sleep. Like that time we fought those Indians coming back from the mine when I was little."

"Silver, you'se know me'se I'se live for this kind of adventure. Good to get out of the leather shop once in a while and see why we'se live a peaceful life in Durango."

"It does make you realize what life is all about protecting loved one and the many friends we have." I reached in my saddlebag and got out two apples and cut them up as we rode and fed them to Blacky and Lagger.

"You boys are doing great this may be our last adventure together but you both will always be on my mind."

We rode on in silent through the dark; the only sound would be when the hoofs of our horses would strike the stones in the trail. We reached a stream that came down the side of the mountain and took time to water the horses and fill our canteens. There were some patches of grass along the stream that the horses grazed on as we rested then we were in the saddle again. The moon was just starting to peek up on the horizon as we came to the long-grade going down into town. But instead of going on down the main street we worked our way around in back of the stables.

"Hand me the three rifles and six boxes of shells BJ and come with me. Foster, you and Peso wait here for us. Then we'll take some of the dynamite to the barn and try to figure out how to get in there."

We took off down the slope and entered the livery from the rear where I knew Orin slept. Martin didn't have the livery guarded. Martin thought he had all the people in town buffaloed by his men but I hoped he was going to find out a different truth this night. If we could get three men up on rooftops just in case we needed backup it would be a big help and in the dark Martins men couldn't tell who was shooting. I opened the door to Orin's room in the livery slowly and looked in and saw Orin snoring on his bunk. I went closer with BJ right behind me and could see Orin face as I reached to put my hand over his mouth and he woke up with a start. I whispered.

"It's me Orin; Buck, we're back to start to give you forks back your town."

Orin sat up and his eyes focused to the dark as he wiped his eyes and stretched to come fully awake.

"Buck, you came back."

"We don't have much time so here's three rifles and shells. If you could get Bill and Simon and get up on the roof to back us up that would help. Then hide the rifles after we leave town for that train coming back from Santa Fe."

"I'll help and I'm sure Bill and Simon will. We're tired of being held hostage in our own town."

"Now don't do any shooting til' you hear a big blast and don't take any chances that will get you hurt. Keep low and hidden and be back in your beds before you're discovered."

Orin was dressed as we left his room and made it out and were on our way up the slope as we saw our first man on guard as we came within a hundred feet of the barn where the rifles were stored. I stopped and watched for a while just to know what we were up against. There were two men that I saw walking round every side of the barn and the barn was locked. They were also carrying lanterns so it was easy to see them. They had to be taken out before we could get in the barn and before daylight. We reached Foster and Peso as we took the dynamite off Josephine and started back down toward the barn.

"Peso, bring your bow and all your arrows we may need you for a silent job."

As we worked our way up over the ridge the moon gave us enough light to see but it also made it more dangerous as we moved among the pines and aspens along the top and the other side of the slope toward the barn. The men that were guarding the barn would meet in front of the barn door as they made their way around the barn and there they would talk and maybe roll a smoke. They looked like they weren't expecting any trouble.

"Peso, you think that you can put an arrow through each man on their next round so they won't yell or make any commotion."

"Me can do, if Buck Taylor not get mad at me for killing white men."

"Not these white men, they are working for a real evil man that wants to start a war between our people. That would mean a lot of killing on both sides."

Peso got two arrows out of his tube and placed one in his teeth and the other on the bow then pulled it back far as he could and waited. Both men were coming around to the front barn door and stopped to talk with lanterns on the ground, which made the light glow up all around them, which gave Peso two perfect targets. He let go with the first arrow and before that arrow struck the first man he had the second arrow on the bow and in the air to hit the second man hard in the chest as the first man was falling dead to the dirt clutching his throat. We four hurried down to the barn with BJ carrying the dynamite and Foster with the fuses. We dragged the two dead men out in the dark behind some boulders then saw we would have to make too much noise to brake the lock.

"Peso, you stay around the corner of the barn and use your bow if anyone approaches the barn and starts to sound an alarm. We're going to try to get in the back loft and blow the rifles and ammunition."

The door in back was locked but the loft was open with a rope coming down.

"Foster, BJ and me will go up and see if any guards are on the inside and try to get this door open without waking the dead. Then you can set the dynamite and light the fuse and we're gone as fast as we can."

"Me'se will wait don't think I'se can get up there."

BJ and me climbed up the rope into the loft and belly crawled to the inside edge of the hayloft that was full of hay which gave us plenty of cover. Down below were two men with pistols at their sides. BJ pointed to himself and signed.

"It's good we learned to talk to Peso. Now I have a way to take them both out at the same time and you jump down after I land."

"You sure about this?" I signed back.

"I got it pa, just you watch and be ready to take care of one of them if they're both not knocked out."

BJ watched the men and looked at the rafters going across the barn and got his bullwhip ready and when both men had their backs to us BJ flung the bullwhip that wrapped around one of the cross beams where they met and he gripped the handle and leaped down toward the men with both booted feet out straight in front of him and caught them square in the chest as they were turning around at the sound of the noise. I made a flying leap down on one man as he was getting up gasping for breath. I knocked him out with a hard punch and the other man was already being tied up by BJ with his own bandana in his mouth. I reached for rope, where BJ had gotten his, and tied my man. I went up to the hayloft with a pickax I found in the corner.

"Here Foster pry the lock off and come in, BJ will get the dynamite." I threw down the pickax to Foster.

"Be me'se pleasure."

The rifles had been placed in a corner of the old barn and covered with canvas like goes on a wagon. We separated the boxes of rifles and Foster said.

"Place two bundles of dynamite in between the cases of rifles and also in between the ammunition. Now get to the door and I'se put the fuses in each bundle and string them to the door and we'se light them and we'se will have a big ka-boom the likes we'se never have seen. More than 4th of July."

"BJ go around and get Peso and as soon as Foster lights this stuff we'll be gone."

"It should give us plenty of time to get to the horses." Foster put in.

Soon as this blew the town's men were going to shoot down some men as they came out from their sleep to see what had happened. Then they would get back to their beds before anyone was the wiser.

This is when Foster lit the fuses and we hightailed it up the slope with BJ and Peso right behind. As we made it to the top of the slope down the ridge to the horses and mounted up we looked back to see the greatest explosion that had ever been seen by anyone of us. As we left the ridge the smoke had started to clear and the barn was nowhere to be seen along with some other outbuildings. No telling how many men were killed cause part of the bunkhouse went up as well and was on fire, the men were running out fanning the smoke away from their face and eyes. There was a man and woman standing in the front yard of the main house with astonished looks on their faces at what just had happened then they turned and the roof of the main house was on fire.

We found the train tracks out a ways from town to the east and we went to following them toward Santa Fe. We moved as fast as we could with the two remaining cases of dynamite staying back away from the tracks in the thick pines. I knew that whoever that was that looked like Dan Walters would be hot on our trail as soon as the town and ranch settled down but that may take some time.

"Peso, could you take BJ and scout our back trail and maybe show him some of the Mescalero's ways of tracking. He's learned quite a bit from Dancing Bear over the years but it's always good to know different ways."

"Go BJ show a lot of our ways." Peso signed.

They left and Foster turned to me.

"How we'se going to get on a moving train?"

"We have time to figure that one out. I hope."

We traveled all day and the day was disappearing to the west and night was slow falling so the shadows of the pines and boulders were getting longer. We stopped to rest the horses beside a creek when Peso and BJ came into the dry camp.

"Me spot men coming, far for now, maybe ten or twelve all together. Rest hour but no more than two. Could not tell they stop for night."

"BJ, you think you can lead me to where you saw them in the dark. Peso you rest your pony here we'll be back in two hours."

"Let's go pa, I can find it."

We headed back down our back trail then BJ turned to the north and then made a large, maybe a half mile, circle to the south then back to the west.

"Peso, showed me that. There are trails different trails from here to our camp. Peso said it would confess them a while till they figured it out."

In an hour we could see a fire burning brightly. They had stopped in a small valley by a stream, which looked to be a perfect place to camp, if you were peaceful cowboys out hunting or rounding up cattle but not what these men were. The valley was surrounded on three sides by high slopes, which made it easy to rain down shells from our repeating rifles sights that were perfect for this work and maybe hit some around the burning fire. They may break camp and start after us but it was worth getting four or five of them so they would be out of the fight. We had boxes of shells with us, and more shells on Josephine. We had two rifles a piece for more firepower. As we started firing we could tell some were hit but others took to the woods. We kept firing into the trees. It sounded like we had started a war and as we rode out fast I knew it would take time for them to get moving again cause we saw some of their horse break away and run who knows how far. They couldn't follow our trail in the dark and when it became daylight the trail would be very confusing. We took a different way back but crossed our other trails two or three times.

When we got back to Foster and Paso they were ready to go. I knew Blacky was tired but he had never failed me in all the years we've been together and well Red he was the young stallion that wouldn't let any horse do more than him. It had always been like that between them. So we went on into the night and then a whistle a ways off in the dark broke the silent.

"Peso is there a bend around here that the train might have to slow down."

"Seen iron horse before, not know of a place like that."

"Well then let's find that track again and see what we find going toward that sound."

"Over here." BJ called out.

We took off east following the train tracks. There would be no problem cause in these mountains they had to make long curves to make it up the grades. Coming up would be a long process more than going down.

"Foster, I watched you in the mine all those years back and back in the barn, that brought back the memories of blasting in the mine so we three will take the two case of dynamite on board and you take the horses on for our get away."

"That sure pleases me'se, didn't know how I'se was going to jump on that moving train."

"Peso, you got your knife and bow and tuck this in somewhere you may need it." I handed him a pistol. He looked at me and nodded his head, he knew what that jester meant.

We were by the tracks, as they would turn up a grade that went among some large boulders then cut into the pines. We would have to move fast to get on and then deal with any men that might be on then set the explosive to take out the whole train and most of the tracks with it.

6

We could see the big one eye monster as Peso called it with that one large light in front with that pipe on top belching out smoke that left a smell of burned wood in the air. We were perched on a huge boulder with the dynamite. I had part of the fuses and BJ had the others as the train came closer. The train had slowed down so much that we nearly could have stepped on but in the dark it became risky. If men were inside the cars they would be on top in no time but we had to risk it. As the engine passed us BJ jumped on the first car and Peso and me passed the cases of dynamite to BJ then we jumped on the second car. The noise bought two gang members from the engine and BJ was ready with his bullwhip. The first man's neck was wrapped with the end of the bullwhip as his gun came out and BJ jerked him and he and his gun went flying over the side in the dark down the mountainside. I passed BJ and caught the second man in the chin with my right fist, which sent him flying and hit hard on the woodpile behind the engine. He was up and BJ's bullwhip passed me and jerked the gun out of the man's hand and the gun fell down in the woodpile. But he came at me again but this time the bullwhip caught him across the face and as he reached for the cut on his face I knocked him over the side screaming till we heard him hit a big pine tree. My gun was in my hand as I told the engineer: "Bring the train to a halt."

"You don't have to tell me twice. But it takes time to stop, I just did this cause they made me that's why the two men were up here. Be careful there's one more in each car. I saw them when they got on." He said, as the wheels started grinding against the metal track and came to a halt in another two hundred feet.

"Leave the train right now and find your way to Flagstaff when dawn breaks. We don't have an extra horse and this train will be gone."

"I'll gladly find my way."

We were now on the ground and I yelled to the men inside. By this time Foster had caught up with us.

"Come out or get blown up with those rifles."

Not a sound from inside.

"Let me'se have that I'se put one stick in the bottom of the door and the doors will fly off. We'se have to get going."

Foster put one stick of dynamite in a hole on each door and lit the fuse. We four ran behind the boulders where Foster had left the horses. When it blew the doors of the train came off their hinges and they splintered to pieces to send debris in all different directions and smoke rose over the whole train. The men stumbled to the doors of each car.

"Martin said not to open the door for anyone till we heard his voice."

"You should have listened to us."

They fell out of the doors flat on their faces they were dead. BJ and Peso drugged the dead bodies away from the train and Foster and me worked on rigging the dynamite up in each car and the locomotive. BJ and Peso came back and we handed each one a case of ammunition to put on Josephine. Then Foster ran the fuses extra-long and when he lit them we made for the horses and made it to the top of the ridge through the pines in the dark. When we reached the top we turned to watch the fireworks. The explosion shook the earth below our feet. The ammunition was shooting in all direction. When the smoke started to clear there was nothing left but rubble of metal and wood. The tracks were turned up on end straight in the air toward the sky. The blast started the trees around the whole area on fire and it was raging toward us.

"I think we've seen enough. Let's make a run for it."

I saw the engineer as we came off the ridge coming down the slope of loose rock. Blacky was handling it well but Red was having a hard time not to lose his footing.

"Hop on in back of me, I'll take you with us a piece away from the fire."

"I hated to see that old locomotive go but that was some blast. I never liked what I was made to do but they had my wife in town and threaten to kill her." He said as we were off through the trees as he held his engineer cap on.

"I hope that Martin and the men that he has left saw that explosion and head that way and maybe Victorio will see it and the two groups will meet there and have a war cause of losing the rifles."

"I'se think that would be a nice ending."

"San Juan, see it and go have real war." Peso signed.

We all started laughing and it sure felt good to laugh again.

After ten miles we left Bob Lang the engineer to walk the rest of the way to town. It was already noon of the next day and the horses needed rest and so did we.

"Bob, start walking after we eat. It's not too far away. Maybe the rifles I left in town will help all you take your town back and here's some extra ammunition we took off the train and two extra rifles. Wrap them up and hide them till the time is right to use them. There can't be that many men left to guard the town. We have to go around they'll be on our trail. Martin's daughter will be there to keep hostage to get Martin to leave."

"What you mean daughter that's his niece. Her father and sister died up north somewhere as I hear tell. Josie was staying with an Aunt somewhere back East when they died. Now Josie refuses to be left alone in town so she won't be in town, always goes with the whole gang."

"Then that has to be Dan Walters daughter. Martin must be Walters brother somehow."

"I heard they were half-brothers same mother different father."

"That's why the different last name. What's Martin first name?"

"Why that a be Jeb Martin."

It was like a lightning bolt had struck Buck. This took Silver Buck back to this man's brother Dan that had killed Buck's great grandfather Jeb more than fifteen years ago. He has the same first name. Foster brought him back to the present.

"Buck, we'se have to get going."

So far we had been lucky to avoid the Mescalero's and the Comancheros that Martin is the head of. We were still in the thick piney forest but as we got closer to the trail of the great canyon the big pines were thinning out with smaller shrub like pines. Then off to the west coming toward us was a cloud of dust.

"Peso, take BJ and see who that is. It may be your friends that put you on that anthill. If you come to William's post let him know what happened. BJ here's some money buy three more cases of 44-40, we might need them."

Peso signed. "If the ones did this to Peso, Peso great surprise for Victorio not so big Chief in Peso's eyes. Lie to son, is no great Chief."

They left and we started to head northwest away from William's post toward the great canyon. Foster knew as we got closer to the trail to the floor of the canyon our trail would be harder to follow cause of the rocky terrain. I would like to see what Peso does when he sees Victorio. That would be a show to pay money to see.

******

Peso and BJ rode off to the west where the thick cloud of dust was filling the air. They left the horses and climbed up a slope where there were giant boulders. Once on top they could see for miles around. They were flat on their bellies with rifles in hand.

Peso signed. "BJ, that Victorio in front, big headdress. He not believe braves that saw me before so Peso will show him in person."

"You think that is wise. He'll really be mad if he sees the truth."

"The only way. Will have more time to get lost from these parts. Victorio will have to think long while, after what he will see what his braves saw."

We when down the rocky slope to the horses and found a creek and Peso got in and dived under the water. He came out and didn't wait to dry off. He jumped in a nearby wallow where some wild horse must have been rolling in. When he came out he had mud from head to toe. Peso held his arms up to the sky what looked like a prayer to his God. I could see he was trying to speak but his mouth would move but no words were coming out and at the same time he went into a dance like I had seen many times in grandfather's village. When this was over he signed to me.

"No speak, but think God know what mean. Now watch from top where will not show self, try to keep from laughing."

He said that cause I already had a smile on my face looking at the way the drying mud looked like dead skin hanging from his arms and legs and every other part of his body.

"Not work, get back to Buck tell Solie go home with new friends make new home for Juan's children among friends of Buck's family."

I worked my way to the top of the rock and laid flat to see what would happen. I had my rifle in case things went wrong I could maybe help him. Peso jumped on the bare back of his pony with a lance in his hand and with a stern face headed toward the huge dust cloud. This man was brave I had no doubt about that. He was riding into what I would think was certain death and he knew it could turn out that way. When he got into range of Victorio he stopped and held up the lance then waved the lance back and forth over his head as the group of Indians came close. He was now signing in a way I hadn't seen before like he was mad at the world. I could now see Victorio in the lead although I had never laid eyes on him before but he was wearing a huge headdress standing up from his head with all the different colors of feathers decorating it.

The group stopped when Victorio raised his lance in the air. All the dust settled down around them as Peso kept ranting on and on in front of the Indians. There may have been two hundred feet between Victorio and Peso. Then Victorio was talking to Peso but Peso only kept ranting in sign. Then he opened his mouth for them to see he still had no tongue to speak with. A strange thing happened when Peso starting riding in a huge circle around the whole group and they just sat there on their pony's and watched Peso go around and around with his lance high in the air. Then he flung it right at the hoofs of Victorio pony and rode off to the north and disappeared from view. Victorio and his braves just sat there looking stunned. By this time ten minutes had passed and the group was starting to mill around Victorio as Victorio raised his lance high in the air over his head as he looked at the lance Peso had thrown and looked to the north where Peso had disappeared then he turned and lead the way south away from the direction Peso had gone. They moved at a fast pace and didn't look back as they went out of my sight.

I crawled away from the top of the boulder and there was Red standing with his ears perked up and out of the brush along the small creek came Peso. He was off and in the creek where he left all the mud then came out with a big smile on his face. He signed. "Still here."

"I watched and didn't believe my eyes. When you threw that lance at Victorio I had my rifle ready to shoot."

"Was an ultimatum? Fight now or leave me go in peace to happy hunting ground. Told disgraced me by the way he murdered a warrior of my place in the tribe and Gods not let in long as pursued me. Get on way, Buck back camp. Solie be worried."

We rode for hours through the pine forest as the pines grow fewer we came to that wonderful sight that we had seen before. There was the trail down to the camp.

"Can tell Buck, Foster with mule down, now we go."

Peso jumped off the pony and brushed out our tracks for a hundred feet and after I took his pony down the trail a ways Peso pulled brush up and made a natural looking barrier blocking the trail down into the great canyon. The trail was tricky all the way down. If we got to close to the edge the dirt would cave off and tumble down in an avalanche. Red was much more sure of his footing than the first time we went down into the canyon. Peso's pony acted like it was normal to have a thousand foot drop off at your side. The sight below us was one of great beauty and a sight many men had not ever seen. The shapes of the pinnacles that seemed to stand all alone straight up from the bottom of the canyon to a point that looked no more than the size of a pencil sticking up five hundred feet or more. Full size pine tree would be growing out of the side of a cliff. The only tree within a thousand feet determined not to fall. Then there were the different colors the red hues and the light blues. There were light shades of colors and then dark shades right on top or bottom of another shade. From the height that we were at you could see the Colorado River on a rampage as it flowed through the canyon with a red color to the water. It was full of brush and some whole trees that had finally ripped away from their home along the bank of the river. As we approached the bottom of the canyon we still could not see the camp for all the brush that filled the canyon along the banks of the river. Even the smoke from a fire could not be seen from where we were coming down. Then we reached the bottom and all I did was follow Peso to the river and along the bank for a few hundred feet and then we saw our whole tribe.

Solie saw us and ran to Peso's side and then Juan was at his father's other side.

"Me all right, Victorio gone not come back for long time. Peso put fear in him that last long time. Not get rifles; big lost to him and fines a ghost was not afraid of him. He was disgraced in front of braves. Long time to live down, most his braves not know he had me murdered. Could see, did not like that to be done to one of theirs and he would not fight me. Only bad white men a problem to us now but Peso has plan. Eat first, hungry for a dead man." Peso signed.

"Peso, do not make joke. You and Juan whole world thought you dead was going to kill myself cause Victorio took Juan away from me also. Had nothing to live for. That why never forget what Buck, Foster and BJ did for my family and me till I die.

"Pa, you should have seen Peso outwit Victorio. Looks like we won't have any more trouble from him for a while. Peso is right about that. You should have seen the way Victorio turn and headed south."

The next morning I went to Peso while we were eating.

"We have to make plans to leave here, but how are we going to get out of here if not up the same trail we came down. I have to meet General Cook on the south end of my ranch to let him know what happened here."

"Have a plan." He pointed to the river and beyond.

"You don't mean we are going to cross that raging river. The horses can't possibly swim that."

"No, you follow me. Know old Indian trail take when young boy. Goes other side of canyon and other trail goes up. Many days before bad men can come around that side." Peso signed.

"They may find the trail coming down here and follow our trail."

"Be gone then and men see the bad river. Think they do not have desire to get us after see the river."

"If Martin is like his half-brother we'll have to fight them sooner are later."

"We fight, see Buck and BJ fight make four of bad men."

Within an hour everything was packed up and Peso lead the way as we followed the raging Colorado. We would come to places where the trail was just wide enough for the horses to pass.

"BJ, here is my telescope I want you to go back a ways to watch our back trail especially the trail coming down and come back fast if you see Martin and his men. We won't cross without you. I'll send Juan when we get to where we cross."

"Will do pa."

We went on and on with the noise of the river always in our ears. Night comes early down in a canyon like this but we moved on after dark as we could still see some light from up above. Peso halted when the stars started to show themselves in the night sky.

"Here we cross in morning. See more by then."

"I still hear the river raging."

"Yes, see in morning this right place I come to two years ago."

There was a sound coming out of the brush and I drew my gun by habit. It was Red coming into view and then BJ. I holstered my gun as BJ came into camp where Solie was cooking and Foster was licking his lips at the smell since we hadn't stopped for dinner.

"BJ, come sit down and have some of this good cooking. Me'se belly been a searchin' for this all the long day and it's about to find it."

Solie laughed as she handed Foster the first plate.

"Solie thinks Foster put on weight since Solie started cooking."

We laughed as BJ took a plate from Solie and said,

"Thank you Solie it looks delicious as all ways but pa we have a problem. I kept a close eye on our trail going all the way up to the top all day. Just before sundown there was movement on the edge of the canyon near our trail. There were two Indians moving brush away from our trail. I stayed till it was totally dark and the fires of their camp could be seen. I couldn't see any more."

"They wouldn't start down the winding trail in the dark but they will start at first light or before."

"San Juan's braves, Mescalero's only one knows trail. See in morning, sure right place. If right, two rafts near use take horses across. One horse, one brave on raft at time, make three time all across. Peso take mule across forth trip know river better."

It was late but crossing the Colorado would not leave my mind so I went for a walk down to the edge of the river. Picking up a rock by habit like I had done many times as a boy in South Texas, I flung it as hard as I could and there was no splash as was expected in my mind. This made me wonder, as another rock was flung across but not as hard as the last time. This time I heard a splash not a thud as last time. It hit dry land the first time for sure I'd bet my bottom dollar on that. This relieved my mind some, if we could find the rafts in the morning things would look rosy so to speak. The river must be less than forty feet across. As I was walking back to our camp in the dark my booted foot hit a bunch of hard dry logs but what would logs be doing down here along the river. A tree wouldn't die this close to abundant water supply. I felt the brush and pulled it away and then felt and there was a raft then not ten feet away there was the other raft. I had to keep myself from waking everyone up I was so happy but tomorrow was going to be a hard day. I found my bedroll and was asleep in less than two minutes. The rest of the night I had dreams about Red Bird and the enjoyment there would be when this was over. As I woke the next morning I could smell bacon and eggs cooking with pancakes and coffee mixed in. This morning I knew things would work out cause every time I had dreams about Red Bird I always returned to her to be held close in my arms.

I walked over to where Solie was cooking. She said to me.

"Men up on rim know we are down here so Solie know we need good breakfast for a hard day work."

"That is true, where is Peso?

"Looks for rafts."

"Found them last night in the dark. Almost broke my foot on them."

As I sat eating Foster, BJ and Juan came to the fire and were eating when Peso came in and sat to eat Solie good breakfast.

"Someone find rafts and vines that tied together, rotten need make more." Peso made his sign.

"No worry Peso, we have plenty of rope to hold them together. Now eat this good food."

"Yes, I eat. All us hurry to work." Peso signed.

I sent BJ and Juan to watch the trail for Martin and his men that I knew would be on our trail as soon as the sun was up in the sky to the east before it reached the bottom of the canyon where we were. We took one rope and cut it into strips after taking the rotten vines off the rafts. Then it was easy to enter weave the rope around the logs which make them nice and tight. Then we tied the two rafts together to make one that was big enough for two horses and two people. I knew that we didn't have time to eat so we started across right away. Peso took Solie and her pony with Josephine the mule, which had all the food, loaded on her back. Peso took the end of another rope tied to his horse and I tied the other end around a huge sphere of rock that was coming out of the ground. Then once on the other side he would tie the rope to another solid object then we could just pull ourselves across the mighty Colorado.

BJ and Juan came riding up fast.

"They are down to the bottom and look to be on our trail." BJ told us as Juan continued.

"Two braves with them. Is why our trail was found on top of canyon."

"You two go next when Peso comes back."

Peso pulled the big raft back across the raging river but not as bad as we had seen back where we had camped.

Peso jumped off the raft. Then said, "Go son, take care of mother."

Red was nervous as BJ pulled him on the raft. He went on as Juan's pony stepped on board. They pulled their selves across and then we saw Juan bring the raft back across. The river was taking its toll on the raft and the ropes were coming lose as white caps of the water was pouring over the raft but Juan made it across just as it started to come apart. We pulled it on shore and tighten the wet ropes as tight as could be.

"Had to come back. Lost once but not again. We go back together or not at all." Juan told his father.

Blacky and me got on the raft with Foster and Lagger next.

"Peso. You and Juan have to come now with us look at the raft it might not make it another time."

I could barely hear my own voice over the crashing of the waves against the rocks in the river.

"We go now Juan." Peso signed.

They got on and we started pulling the raft across the Colorado then about three quarters of the way across the raft started to break up as I told Peso and Juan to get on Lagger and Foster and me got on the back of Blacky just in time as both horses jumped into the raging waves of water that was pouring over us. We came up to see the raft break to pieces on the boulders down river. Peso and me grabbed the rope as the horses heads broke the top of the water and started swimming for shore. When we came closer to shore I took my huge knife that I always carry and started cutting the rope in pieces and Blacky and Lagger walked on shore with all four of us on their backs.

Solie came running to the shore of the river and took Peso and Juan with her with tears in her eyes. I looked at Foster.

"Looks like you got your bath early this year."

"Now Silver, you'se knows I'se changed when Juanita came to keep house for me'se."

"I know but it's nice to be alive after that river ride."

Blacky and Lagger were shaking the water from their backs then went to roll in the grass. I opened the saddlebag and got two apples out and went to cutting them in pieces. I took them over to Blacky and Lagger.

"Boy's you deserve this and all our thanks."

I was rubbing their heads and down their mane getting the water off the coats when Solie came over and put her arms around Lagger's neck.

"Thank you Lagger for bringing my men safe to me. Buck Taylor I do not know what drives you but thank you for believing in Peso. What Juan did for his father made him a man in my eyes and will be a kind and gentle man as his father."

She hugged me around the neck with tears of joy running down her face.

"Solie, Juan is a man in my eyes as well. Your family will have a great life once we get back home."

Before we could look back at the ragging Colorado River there came bullets flying over our heads and ricocheting off the boulders around us.

"Solie, hurry now, take the horses and mule back aways from this."

Foster and BJ brought the rifles and ammunition up and Peso and Juan were right behind them. "We don't have time to get out of here right now; maybe we can pick off some of Martin's men before we pull out. They can't try to get across if they're busy ducking our bullets."

We took up positions behind boulders along the shore as bullets flew all around us. Then it was our turn as we started firing back across the river, which made them take cover. I could see Martin and the woman I knew to be Josie Walters. I yelled across the river as loud as was possible not knowing if he could hear me or not.

"Martin, just let us go on our way and you won't hear from us again."

"Are you kidding, you spoiled my deal with Victorio and San Juan worth hundreds of thousands of dollars in gold and they know where more gold is and I'm going to know to, once you're out of the way. After I'm through with all of you, you won't be bringing any army down on us."

"I don't know what you're talking about we just didn't like you selling rifles to the Indians to kill more people. We were on our way home."

"You really want me to believe that."

Then I heard another voice and knew it was Josie.

"We know who you are now, you're the one that killed all my family."

"Josie, I didn't kill any of your family except your brother and it was a fair fight."

"Go to Hell Silver Buck."

7

The bullets started flying again and Josie fired the first shot of this round and the bullets came might close to our heads as we ducked behind the boulders again. I turned around to talk to Peso and he was nowhere in sight. I looked at Solie back with the horses and she pointed to the cliff back behind us. As I looked there in the lens of my telescope I could see Peso and Juan climbing up the side to the top of the cliff. I saw they both had rifles with boxes of ammunition and their bows and arrows across their backs.

"Foster, BJ fire away try to keep them busy so they can reach the top."

We stopped firing when I saw they had reached a place with plenty of cover to protect them both. They took their bows first and started their attack with the first two sets of arrows hitting their targets as screams came to us on the air from the other side of the river. Four more men were now out of the fight as Martin's men spotted where the arrows were coming from and started firing at the cliff but with no hits. Peso and Juan laid down their bows and started firing at the other side of the river with their rifles with two more men going down. This drove Martin's men back further from the river to take cover from the bullets that were raining down on them from above. From where Peso had drove them back to, we were almost out of their firing range.

"Foster, BJ get to the horses, this is our chance to get away. It's going to take Martin a long while to get across."

I got Peso attention and signed him.

"Will leave your horses around the backside of the canyon. We'll take Solie with us. You made a good dent in their men. Maybe they'll turn back. Catch up to us as soon as you can to lead us out of this canyon."

As we all mounted BJ took Peso and Juan's horses and tied them. They were firing across the river when we followed Solie through the winding canyon. I looked a last time and saw Peso and Juan coming down the backside of the cliff. Martin and his men were coming to the river's edge and firing but we were out of their range cause of the winding trail. Peso was with us in no time and took the lead through the canyon. He signed to us;

"Take one more sunrise be out of canyon. Where I go is hard to follow plenty rock no soil to leave hoof prints."

As we rode I passed around the jerky for we couldn't stop to have a meal for who knows how long. The night was coming on and we were still on Peso's heels then he pulled up and there in front of us was water bubbling out of the rocks with a large patch of grass for the horses. As we rested Peso came over and signed.

"Many moons since was here. Not many know this place look same. Lucky water still runs and grass still grows."

"Looks like our horses won't leave much grass for our followers. Maybe they won't come close to here."

"They'se will be tired after crossing the river and will have to rest their horses maybe all night. They'se can't follow our trail at night." Foster put in.

"Sleep some and we will go. Son and me will keep watch."

We all fell to sleep under the moon lit cloudless skies. The horses were happy with the grass and water nearby. Then in two hours we were on the trail again with canyon walls reaching hundreds of feet above our heads.

"Pa, Juan and me been talking and if we stay back up on those cliffs with your telescope we can get a glimpse of them before they can get close. Juan says he can follow his father's trail. We'll go up before sunrise."

"That will be helpful but be sure to tie the horses so they won't run off."

The break of dawn was starting to set the surroundings on fire with its light and BJ and Juan stayed back as we went on. As we turned the next curve the boys were half way up where the sun would hit them first. It was five hours and we were coming out of the north side of the canyon when the boys caught up to us. I could see they had been riding hard. We stopped and they told us what happened. First Juan came out all excited.

"Two hours we sit there and then we saw them in the distant." Then BJ interrupted.

"I got this idea after looking at the rocks around us for those two hours." Then Juan interrupted.

"BJ took his bullwhip and whipped at the rocks and they fell to the bottom on the trail we came." Then BJ;

"So I got that bullwhip a cracking and before we knew it the trail was ten feet deep and about twenty feet wide cause every time some rocks rolled down it set more and more rolling down the cliffs all around us." Then Juan;

"No other way to go around for miles as we saw. Will take long time to get the horses over that slide."

"Good job boys. That will gain us some valuable time. Peso, we're going to meet General Cook at the south end of my ranch I think it's northeast of here."

"Know way, is Ute country but say wife's father is good so will go." Peso signed.

"Dancing Bear will make you at home when he hears your story. His people live in the foothills of the mountains north of my ranch but one day his future people will have all the southern part of my ranch with my children with the northern part. It is written down for white man's courts."

We were now up out of the canyon on a plateau. The trees of Flagstaff were all but gone and the landscape was more like that of the canyon. There was no way we could go on without some rest. Peso found a spot back in a small, wooded area hidden with a spring and some grass. Solie cooked our first meal in two days. We sat around the fire eating then everyone got some much-needed rest for most of the night till we were woken up by the sound of hoofs far off in the night. The fire had been put out after we ate so no one could tell we were here till they rode up on us. We had hobbled all the horses close by. The sound was coming closer and getting louder so we decided to saddle up and leave. As we rode out Peso came to me and signed.

"No horses heard before not for long time. No men but buffalo." As he signed the noise became louder. There were boulders with space for us all to fit. The noise was more intense and we were off our horses and up on top by the time dawn was coming we could see a sea of black for what seemed like miles. Mothers with their calves and the huge bulls that locked horns once in a while but they had settled down and were eating the sparse grass that there was. Peso signed.

"Is good, wipe out tracks for miles. Work way through slowly and not start stampede."

We headed out into the herd of buffalo slowly. They parted as we went on like they didn't know we were there. No words were spoken all day and into the night till we found a spot as the buffalo drifted more to the south and away from us. We ate and slept all night till the light hit our eyes but as I opened my eyes to the morning sun there was Solie cooking and Peso was up on a boulder looking out over the horizon.

"Solie, don't you two sleep."

"Not much, Peso says came close to sleeping all ways and says rather be awake for now. Want to make a good home for Juan and me and hope will find it with Buck Taylor and friends. Says has to protect Buck Taylor even with life."

"That's not why I took care of him but you did most of the doctoring not me."

"No argue, Peso knows Buck Taylor took off anthill what come later no matter. Would be dead by ants before Solie could be there."

The day was bright with the sun in a cloudless sky that let all the goodness of life be felt down deep in one's soul. Peso was out front with Solie riding behind him. He was sure a warrior that never faltered and knew where he was going even if he had never been there before. Juan and BJ were on our back trail watching for Martin and his Comancheros. They had become friends and liked to know that they had a role to play in this long journey, then Foster and me in the middle with Josephine the mule. It had been cool days and cold night down in the canyon but now out in the open of the full sun it was becoming hot as the desert south of the canyon. We stopped to rest at noon to eat and rest the horses beside a bubbling creek that was a good mile off the trail we had been on. Peso and his pony seem to always know where the water and grass were. As we sat eating and Solie had taken the boys their food up on a boulder where they were on lookout, I ask Peso:

"I take it that you know where we're going. I've never been this way till now." He signed.

"Peso knows, small town not far go around. White man name Tuba City, we go on Navajo trail, go north no trouble with Navajo. Turn way sun rises two more suns, close to Ute country hope no trouble."

"I think Foster and me have to go into this Tuba City and get some supplies. Not much large game in this country. Wish we could have risked and shot a buffalo that would have lasted."

"Town where sun set from here."

"You four go on we'll catch up by night."

Foster and me started out for Tuba City with a light pack on Josephine. We had left most of our supplies with Peso. Going toward town the trail was pretty well worn by traveling wagons. When we came to the main street we saw a saloon and a general store all in one building with no paint and it looked like it was most about to fall down. At the hitching rail there were three horses tied with the reins hanging in the dirt below. The horses had been ridden hard, there was lather all foamed up on their coats. The men that rode them didn't care at all about their horses for they tied them ten feet away from a water trough. We tied our horses at the water trough and I untied the three horses and led them toward the water so they could drink.

"Silver you'se think you'se should be doing that."

"It riles me to see good horses treated like this."

I was taking them back to tie them up when three men stepped out of the saloon doors. Two were dirty, and I don't mean from just being out on the trail for weeks but they had beards with food left from them eating and with greasy hair sticking out from under their hats. The third man was clean cut with a smile on his face with two low hanging guns at his sides.

"What you think you're doing with our horses?" The man with the big smile said in a nice way.

"Your horses seem to need some of that refreshing water and they took kindly to being led to it. I guess you had something more important on your mind."

"We will give them water when we think they need it."

"Look mister I don't want any trouble just being neighborly. There's no water within miles of here and what would you do if your horses died right under you."

"I'se told you'se Buck." Foster whispered.

"Go on inside and get what we need I'll take care of this."

Foster hurried off inside and I retied their horses where they had been.

"Where's the old man going?"

"That's really none of your business but we're on the trail and need some supplies, if you really care. We don't like to go without food just as much as your horses don't like to go without water."

"You think you can take all three of us."

"Well, if those friends of your take as much care of their guns as they do of their self then I'd say yes. I did nothing but trying to give your poor horses a drink of water. Some people would have thanked me."

"But I'm not in a thankin' mood right at this moment. You see."

He made his move and I could see it in his eyes so that gave me a split-second advantage. My gun was out and firing by the time he cleared leather. He laid on the front porch of the saloon as I turned toward the other two that had their hands up in the air as my gun was pointed in their direction.

"Si senor, we thank you with all our hearts."

"Si, me to. What he said."

"Get down your hands and get your buddy across his horse and get out of here. Pronto!"

"Si, Si we are gone like ghost."

I walked in the store to find the storekeeper trying to get our order together and was saying.

"I could see those three were nothing but trouble as soon as they came through those doors. Demanding this and that and me not having the right kind of liquor they wanted. I thought I was surly in trouble."

"Have you seen them before?"

"Not without their boss and he's even worst. I could do without their business."

"Boss, what does he look like?"

"Just older with grey in his hair but he has a good-looking niece. Of course my wife helps her. You know how it is with wife's."

"Foster, get double what we thought we needed and get everything tied to Josephine and we'll get out of here. Mister don't watch us leave that way you can't tell them which direction we went when they come back with their boss."

We threw our leg over our saddle and rode away in a different direction than we had come into town and when we were out of sight of town we circled around to the right direction as we drugged brush behind us to cover our tracks some.

"Foster, we can't go into any more towns, Martin must have men in every little burg around these parts."

"Since he knows who you'se are he may figure out where we'se are headin'."

"It might be good if he follows us all the way to the ranch where General Cook will be."

"You'se know that Martin is a slick one, if he does figure that out and sees Cook before we'se can get there he may be able to convince Cook that you'se turned bad and are selling rifles to the Indians yourself. You'se told him in that canyon that we were headin' to the ranch."

"You know Foster sometimes you amaze me. Let's hurry I have to try to figure out what to do next. Seems we have to send one or two to get to the ranch first and warn General Cook about Martin."

By the time we rode into camp the shadows were long and deep and the camp had already been set up for the night. As we set around eating Foster and me explained what had happened in town and what we suspected Martin might do. "I'm going to think about the situation overnight and in the morning we will have to send one or two of us to meet General Cook." Peso spoke up with his signs.

"Me know the way, go. Tell Juan go toward where wind blows in cold season and where sun comes up he will lead to home."

"That make some sense but Foster, BJ or me will have to go with you to explain to General Cook. You know some white men; he may not believe you if you're alone after what happened to Custer at the Little Big Horn."

"Buck Taylor thinks good. Go with one of you, Juan get you home. All can live in peace."

"Let's hope so Peso."

That night was long for I could not sleep thinking about which one of us to go with Peso. I looked over and there was Peso drawing in the dirt showing how Juan was to lead the group home. Juan looked to be taking it in very seriously and watching intently to what his father was explaining. I drifted off with my head still full of my thoughts. Then from deep inside my brain came Red Bird. She was talking to me.

"Buck Taylor, as you told me before you left we can't keep BJ as our little boy. If my father was the kind of Chief that fought all the time BJ would be a warrior at his age and already count many coups and maybe killed many men. He is of our blood and has in him the will to survive anything that might come his way. As his mother I do not want to see any harm come to him but I also want to see him become the man that his father is and I know it is deep inside of him. I love you very much and I know you and BJ and even old Foster will come back safe to us."

As I opened my eyes to the break of dawn it was like a great weight had been lifted off of my shoulders. The night was short but I seemed to be fully rested as I sat up to empty out my boots and pull them on. BJ came to me all excited as Solie handed me a plate of food.

"Well pa, have you made up your mind who is going with Peso. I know I'm young but I know the job is for me to do. Peso and me have become close friends and we can handle any trouble that comes our way."

By then Peso had come to sit down and listen to what I was going to say.

"I think you and Peso can handle this and I trust him with my life and yours. Your mother thinks you can handle this to. So if Solie will pack you two food for the trail you two better get going before that sun comes up." Peso signed.

"Red Bird came during night. Know how is when woman loves her man."

"Yes, she did Peso. She reminded me what her father would do if he was a warring Chief and BJ would already be a warrior in the tribe and he has to become a man for himself." BJ had Red saddled and was saying they had to leave and get to General Cook as Solie handed him a bundle of food that he put behind his bedroll and Peso jumped on his bareback pony and they headed northeast away from us and we four mounted and headed the same way at a slower pace with Juan in the lead. I watched them as they disappeared from our sight and I saw Solie watching the same as me.

******

I knew now that my pa knows I am a man of my own now that he had let me go on beside Peso to do such an important job as this was. It was not my way to think that there was no danger for we had some bad Comancheros somewhere out here and Peso says that we could never know what Victorio would do. I had a dream last night and I know not why but the memory of that river crossing came back to me and the beautiful woman with that long red hair that was yelling at pa about him killing all her family from across that river. I know that my pa could never have done what she was yelling about he just is not that kind. I couldn't get a clear view of her but I know she was beautiful by the way she looked as she moved when she was angry. I guess she couldn't be much older than me but I couldn't be sure from that distant.

I came out of my reverie as Peso took a turn down into an arroyo that led to a chain of small ravines that led to a small creek that could not had been seen from above. We watered our horses here and ate a small meal as the horses fed on a small patch of grass that had grown up around the creek. Peso signed.

"Now know BJ has Indian blood, warriors do not speak much as ride on trail."

"Peso, I think of you as a friend and you would tell me the truth. Do you think a woman can be told wrong all her life and later change when she finds out the truth?" Peso signed.

"Could, Solie thought she loved a brave that was high up with tribe. Saw her and know she only one for me but was of no important till one night went north raid horse ranch. Rancher's men came out before we could get most of his horses but I had five horses when we rode back into village and other brave that Solie liked only had one. Horses like gold in our world and five horses made me a bigger man in eyes of all our people. Saw Solie look at me in a different way after that. Ask Solie if her father take five horses for her to be my wife. Solie say maybe two more and gave me big smile. Next night Peso went out alone to different ranch and next morning came to Solie lodge with nine horses and ask her father for Solie to be mine for always. Solie was standing behind her father smiling and looking so beautifully shy."

"Well, what happened?"

"See Solie with me now and have great son. Go on now, sun high in sky."

He lead off down one of the ravines that came up on the plateau that we had been on all morning. The afternoon was hot and the sweat was rolling down the back of my neck as the sun went across the sky to be lost in the west behind the mountains as we came to a little creek that would do us and the horses for the night. Peso always found a place that was hidden from the trail. I built a small fire with the dry brush that was around, so there wouldn't be much smoke raised up for anyone to see, to cook our meal while Peso was out looking for some game. He came back with a small antelope and we had a great meal as night closed in around us so I got in my bedroll and Peso climbed up on ledge and laid down. He seemed to always be on watch.

After we ate in the morning we left by a means I had not seen before. Instead of going up on the plateau like the two days before Peso took us through a series of ravines that twisted and turned for seemed like miles. Down here there was no breeze or it seemed like not even much air to breathe. It was so hot that we could just about cook on the top of one of the boulders that were all round us sticking up toward the sky like pillars of the community. Then Peso held up his hand in a sign for me to stop and he went on around the next boulder. He must have heard a sound that was not usual and that I didn't hear. Peso came back and signed for me to come and as I moved Red forward someone leaped on Red behind me and grabbed me around the throat as I started to yell for Peso he put a knife to my throat. As he tighten his grip I saw two Mexicans jump Peso knocking him to the ground as they landed on top of him and Peso fought hard against these two but then two Indians appeared with ropes and bound his hands and feet. The two Indians came and bound my hands but the one behind me stayed where he was but took the knife from my throat as Red started to resent two people on his back and reared up but the two with the ropes jump and held onto Red around his neck as Red flared up high and came down hard jerking them hard but not enough to shake them loose. Red settled down for he couldn't shake them. They threw Peso over his pony and they led us to the top of the plateau as the man behind me took up my reins from behind. We rode where we went on through the heat and dust for an hour or two.

We then came to a spot with plenty of shaded trees and a stream flowing by but there were also more Indians and Mexicans scattered around along the banks of the stream and more under the low brushy trees. There were women also with Mexican and Indian men all over them with bottles of whiskey in the other hand that wasn't busy pawing the woman next to them and dirty, they looked like they hadn't bathe in a year, even the women, with a creek right next to their camp. The men's beards had food left in them from breakfast and the hair of both men and women were so tangled and dirty that a comb or brush hadn't been near their head. The Mexican that was behind me now I knew from watching his dark sleeved arms and hands for hours holding the reins in front of me. He now jumped off Red and pulled me to the ground and as I hit the ground hard I was watching them pull Peso from his pony and they tied us both to a tree back-to-back on opposite sides of the tree. Then I saw a white man come out of a shelter that had been built against a boulder that stood under one of the few tall trees it had some kind of makeshift door that closed behind him as he came toward us so it couldn't be seen what was inside. He stepped in front of Peso and I heard him.

"Where are you taken this boy and where is Silver Buck and the old man."

Peso couldn't say a word and wouldn't even if he could so I heard him slap Peso across the mouth.

"Martin, he can hear you but he can't speak he has no tongue to speak with so no use hitting him."

He came around to my side of the tree and looked me straight in the eyes.

"So you know who I am but you see that you call me Mr. Martin."

"I only call men Mister that I respect and you're not one of them."

He took his backhand to my face. It made me mad cause this was the first time I had been hit without being able to defend myself. The other times it was only schoolmates that had a disagreement with something I had said defending my grandfather's people.

"Untie my hands and try that again and see what happens."

"Kind of feisty for a young pup. I bet you know how to use that bullwhip that my men took off of you? I'll ask you since you are the one able to talk, what is your name and where were you two going and where's Silver Buck?"

I did not answer and he hit me again and I could feel my face turning red not from the slap but from the anger but I knew from what my pa said "Don't let them see you angry" to act nice and calm.

I smiled right in his face as blood I could taste ran down the side of my mouth.

"You think that hurt, try something else maybe it will feel better."

I could see he was angry now but I had to keep them from hurting Peso if I could he had already been through enough.

"Get me his bullwhip, now!"

The man that had been sitting behind me brought my bullwhip to Martin.

"Now we'll see if this will loosen your tongue."

They untied me and turned me so my face was toward the tree my face scrapping the tree's bark and my back was facing Martin as I could hear the whip pop loud in my ears. They tore my shirt from my back so there would be nothing between my bullwhip and me except my bare back.

8

"Stop Uncle Martin. That is to cruel even for you."

"What are you doing Josie? You know how I operate. He'll tell me what I want to know and we'll swoop down on the man that murdered your family."

"I said no Uncle and I mean it. Tomas untie the young one and take him to my tent."

I spoke up. "No, not unless you let my friend loose to. I rather take the whip."

Tomas spoke to Martin. "This one seems to be brave. What should I do?"

"Uncle I'll leave you when I get a chance if you touch either one of them."

Martin looked puzzled and was standing next to me rubbing his bare chin with his fingers like he was thinking hard about what he should do.

"Yes, I see your point Josie that red hair of yours is now showing in your temper."

"You taught me well uncle."

"Tomas, do as she says but tie both of their hands behind their backs and their feet together. No food and water. Pronto!"

"And so you'll know uncle you sleep out here with your men and that whore you brought to the tent and took to bed last night and were you thinking of auntie at the time. She thought you were so true to her when you left to come west from Boston."

"Now Josie a man needs his pleasures at times and your aunt having been dead all these years."

"But not in the tent not five feet from my bed. I don't care how long she's been died what you did maybe unforgivable. Just you remember sleep out here."

"I'll not have you in that tent alone with those two. Tomas you get some sleep now and stay in front of that tent all night and don't go to sleep."

"Si, Senor. Tomas understands."

Tomas took us to the tent against the boulders. I was trying to think of a way of escape as Tomas was tying our hands and feet. Tomas left the tent and no one came in so I started to whisper to Peso next to me in the darkness of the tent.

"I know you can't answer me but we have to get out of here and get to General Cook before they find our family."

Peso was trying to speak but gave up and shook his head yes. Then he was rolling his eyes from left to right and his head from left to right and looking up toward the top of the tent. I didn't understand for the longest time but then it dawn on me.

"You think we'll get our chance to get out of here tonight after the sun goes down."

He shook his head yes and then the strangest thing of all. Peso puckered his lips and nodded his head toward Josie bed.

"Peso, I'm not going to try to bed her."

He shook his head no but then he moved his lips and moving his head.

"I get it, talk nice to her and say things she'll want to hear that she hadn't heard since her aunt died."

Once again Peso shook his head yes and I never seen him so excited as at this moment. I stopped talking as the flap of the tent opened and that beautiful redhead, Josie walked in as the sunshine came streaming through the opening. It was like a halo around her whole body and beautifully shaped head. She left the flap open till she lit the lamp then she closed the flap and tied it. Then she spoke.

"Don't talk to loud, I don't want them to hear us talking."

"What are you doing with this band of thieves? They get many people killed by selling guns to the Indians. You just don't seem like that kind of woman to be running with these barbarian people. Out there talking to your uncle you didn't seem like the same person that was yelling at my pa across the river. I thought back at the river that anyone that beautiful and with that bright red hair couldn't be that bad to think my pa would just kill with no regard for anyone."

"So you are Silver Buck's son. I just knew you had to be when I saw you up close for the first time. I had heard tales from my aunt about how Silver Buck had found his silver mind and the stories were told in the newspapers how handsome he was. My aunt read them to me when I was about four, the articles were already years old. There were also pictures of my father and I thought he looked so much like my uncle only older. I asked my aunt and she laughed and said that is why she married him cause he looked so much like my father and she just adored my father since she had been little."

I looked over at Peso and he was shaking his head yes as I kept on buttering her up.

"I heard about such articles but they had told me that the articles told of the trial of your father and how your sister died falling off a cliff accidently pushed by your father and your brother was killed in a fair fight by my pa. I am BJ his son but you seem so refine and nice to be here. How did you come to be with these people that kill and murder?"

"I guess my aunt left out the bad parts because I was so young. I was born late in life for my mother and she died when I was born. My brother and sister were a lot older so my father left me with my aunt and uncle in Boston and went west to make his fortune with my brother and sister. He was already a lawyer and thought he would do better out here where the law was not in many places so a lawyer would be needed to protect people from wrong doers. That's what I was told and then my uncle got a letter from father that told of how my father was getting rich and my uncle Jeb should come help him set up a new deal he was planning. That's what he told my aunt anyway. My aunt didn't want him to go help her brother because she had been so ill. He went anyway saying the money would come for the doctor to make my aunt well and then we could come west to join him and I would be with my family again."

"Can you untie our hands? Peso can only talk with his hands. I know how hard it has been for you and to leave Boston when all the young men that must have been around you all the time being the way you look."

I was telling her this as she untied our hands and got the circulation going again in our hands as I rubbed them. Then she went on with her story.

"That's not true. I hardly ever went out because it was my duty I thought to take care of my sick aunt and then last year she died and I was left all alone. I stayed with my aunt's friends until my uncle wrote to us after he got word of her death. He said for me to come west and live with him. So I had to because he was my only relative that I knew of. I only arrived two months ago. These people around him I didn't like but I had no choice. I made a friend of Tomas; he will do almost anything for me. I think he's kind of smitten with me."

"Why did you change your mind from what you thought of my pa when yelling at him across the river in that great canyon?"

"For two months my uncle had been filling my mind with the way my family had been murdered by Silver Buck and my father's silver mine had been stolen by him. I only knew what my aunt had told me about Silver Buck finding a silver mine so this was all new to me and it made me madder the more I thought about it. Then when Silver Buck blow up my uncle's train with the guns and the barn full of guns all to sell to the Indians and your pa told us across the river how bad my uncle was getting people killed by the Indians I started to think." Peso signed.

"Bad Indians, want war all time kill white man. Told to many have to make peace learn to live along side of white man. Do this to me." I told her what he had said then he opened his mouth to show Josie how bad some of his people are. She looked and covered her face with her hands and turned her head away and I could see tears come to her eyes.

"How cruel can people be?"

"That is our reason for destroying the guns." She continued and we listened intently.

"That night in camp I looked around and saw all the women and men around me how depraved they were and then my uncle brought that woman to my tent. I thought he must have drunken to much but he didn't seem to be drunk as I watched the going on. I couldn't take it anymore so I had it out with him. He finally admitted the truth about your father but we would be rich yet. So I'm here to help you get away if you will take me with you BJ. I can't stay with him anymore. I can find work somewhere and live on my own. I just know it can be done."

"Peso thought we could escape tonight but your uncle has Tomas out in front of the tent all night."

"Don't worry I can take care of that if you take me with you."

"How could I say no to a beautiful woman as you."

She blushed as deep as her red hair and she started to leave the tent. I stopped her by asking.

"Can you get our guns and horses and my bullwhip? I made it myself in Foster's leather shop back home in Durango."

"Wait, till after dark and the camp settles down when they are all drunk with their liquor." She was talking as she came back to untie our feet.

We moved around the tent more freely but kept an eye out through the tied door. It was late afternoon and Tomas was already coming from down by the creek leading his horse. When he was almost to the front of the tent I saw Josie stop him and talk for a few minutes and then he came and tied his horse to a limb of a tree in front and sat down on a stump across the way. Josie had headed to a roll of tents that stood down by the cool looking creek that had the late afternoon sun rays gleaming off the still nice cool water. That just reminded me that we hadn't had any food or water since this morning. I hoped Red and Peso's pony were being taken care of. Then Peso saw Tomas coming our way so we sat and wrapped the ropes around our ankles and got our hands tucked back behind our backs just as Tomas walked through the flap of the tent. He looked at us and smiled showing all his shining white teeth with his black mustache drooping down on each side of his mouth. His eyes were gleaming as he threw his sombrero off his head to his back to be hanging by the cord around his neck. He spoke to us now as he bent to check our ropes around our ankles. Then his smiles got even bigger.

"So senora Josie tells me some of the truth. You are loose and are still here. Are you who she says you are?"

"Who would that be?"

"Answer me cause it depends on what you say if I can do as she wants me to do tonight."

"If Josie told you I am Silver Buck's son then she was telling you the truth. My name is BJ."

"You are young and may be a fool for I could go tell Senor Martin who you are and I might get a large reward for finding that out."

"But if you did that Tomas, Josie would hate you forever and wouldn't want you close to her anymore. She has said she likes you very much."

"You are not such a fool as I had thought. This I know and you seem to know what is inside my heart and brain."

I looked at Peso and he looked at me and we both brought our hands from behind our backs and stood up. I asked Tomas.

"Why do you want to help us Tomas?"

"Not to ever have to face the law and a good job at your father's ranch that I have heard so much about and to be close to Senorita Josie to serve her when she needs me. I used to be a very good vaquero down in old Mexico many years ago before the revolution. That's when I became what I am today but I was young and thought it was the way to change my country for the better but now Tomas is getting older and sees this is not a good way to live out one's life. I want a life of peace."

"Tomas, this I promise will happen if you help us tonight. That is the same reason that Peso is helping us so he can start a new life for his family."

"Then till late tonight your horses will be ready along with Senorita Josie's and she has told me you want your guns and here is your bullwhip I had it on my horse. I never gave it back to Senor Martin when he was going to have me whip you in front of everyone. Your guns will take a little looking to find them so if I am late leave with Senorita Josie and I will try to catch up in the dark. But make sure she is safe away from her uncle for he is very cruel."

Tomas left us standing there in the middle of the tent untied. Peso signed to me.

"See has a love for girl and means will not let us down. See it in eyes."

"I see that to and will keep my promise to him."

"Have to wait. Sun go down soon. Girl come and we leave fast not stop soon."

"I hope they took care of our horses and left the food in our saddlebags."

"Think girl likes you and will take care of all that before night. Thinks BJ likes girl."

"You see and know too much Peso." Then I smiled.

We paced back and forth in the tent and kept a lookout through the tied tent door. Then the sun went down behind the boulders as the fires started to blaze in the twilight just before the dark curtain of night fully surrounded us. Then we were in total darkness inside the large tent. I sat and relaxed better now that dark had fallen and no one else had come in to check on us. The noise could be heard starting to get louder and louder as the night grew later. We could see two fires from the tent but there seemed to be many more for we could see the glow in the sky, and the women were dancing around the fires to entertain the men that seemed to be pulling at the bottles of liquor. The liquor and the girls seemed to keep them busy and their minds off us. I had to lie down and try to get some sleep and Peso did the same after wrapping the ropes loose around our legs and our hands behind us as we lay back-to-back on our sides.

I woke up not knowing how long I had slept but Peso was not beside me anymore. Then I heard a small noise toward where the flap of the tent was and I crawled on my hands and knees to the flap in complete darkness and there I found Peso keeping watch as always. I was close enough to see Peso sign.

"Many sleep few on guard. Not seen Tomas or girl."

"I hope I was right to tell them as much as I did but it may have been our only chance to get away."

"This is true."

Then we heard some movement to the side of the tent. It sounded like a horseshoe hitting against rock. We hurried and laid down like we were still tied. I managed to hide my bullwhip under a blanket that was on Josie's bed. The flap of the tent came open and the low glow of the remaining fires could be plainly seen as a figure came in the opening toward us. It wasn't till the figure bent down to loosen our bounds that I could see it was Josie. I told her.

"No need for that we are still loose."

"Then let's be out of here, get low around the edge of the tent for my uncle still has guards down away from the fires and there is one that Tomas is taking care of out on the trail north."

"Now did you know we are going north."

"Tomas says your ranch is north in Colorado."

She said this as we left the tent, I went by Josie's bed to grabbed my bullwhip. No guard was near the tent for they heard Martin tell Tomas to guard the tent all night. As we rounded the corner of the tent low as we could I saw beside the back of the tent Red and Peso's pony alongside Josie's mare. As we came nearer I saw that all our weapons were on the saddle. I put my hand over Red's mussel for I knew he would nay as he sensed me close and then I handed Peso his rifle and I buckled on my six-gun and tied it down and my rifle was already in the scabbard. I helped Josie in her saddle and then I was on Red and Peso led the way slowly out of camp as it became darker away from the small light that were left of the fires as they were let to burn out toward dawn that was a few hours away. We were going to have to put as many miles between this camp and sunrise, when someone would discover we were gone, as we could before they were on our trail and no doubt they would be for we had Martin's niece and his right-hand man.

As Peso increased the speed we were traveling as now the moon was rising above the trees and the many boulders so the trail could be seen clearer as it was a bright full moon with stars in the clear cool night. Then as we rounded one boulder a rider came out of nowhere and blocked our trail. Then I saw the many white teeth in that smile that I knew to be Tomas.

"That guard will not ever sound an alarm again." That was all he said as he moved in beside Peso in the led with Josie and me behind.

We had been moving fast now for hours and as dawn came upon us from out of the east Peso as always found a creek with grass for the horses and we stopped to rest and eat our first small meal in two days and fill our canteens with that cold fresh water.

"Peso, we need to hurry with Martin on our trail and General Cook waiting for pa at the south end of our ranch. Pa may run right into Martin and his men so as soon as we make contact with General Cook we'll head back to help my Pa and your family with old Foster. This country is starting to look familiar to me."

"Have to let horses rest, eat and drink till full and girl needs rest not use to trail ride." He signed as BJ told Josie.

"Peso that's nice of you but I'll be alright and won't hold you back."

"BJ sees more he knows; BJ will take led to where General is. Talk to General keep Tomas and Peso out for now. Later when BJ explains and family is safe Peso led General to Victorio stronghold."

"You can led General Cook to round up Martin and his men as we find Pa and the rest."

We were there going on two hours went we were mounted and on our way again. The rest of the day was hard on Josie but she held up and did not complain one bit as we came closer to our goal and home. That night we stopped by the river that bound our ranch's southwest side and I knew the General should be near now. We slept this night better than any other night but I woke up and Peso and Tomas were not in camp. Just before sunrise Peso came riding in from the east and Tomas came riding in from the south as Josie and me were cooking breakfast and threw up a cloud of dust as they both dismounted. We handed them a plate of food and they ate it down fast and Tomas kicked out the fire with his boots and Peso signed.

"General where sun comes up maybe three miles. Peso gets close." Then Tomas spoke in a rush.

"Martin and men not more than half day ride. I didn't get very close for I might not have come back for they did not stop last night."

Josie and me were packed and mounded in five minutes and across the river in another five. I was in the led now for this was the ranch where I grow up and was my home and Josie was right beside me as we came over the next rise and saw the General's encampment. We stopped and Peso signed.

"BJ, girl go see General, Tomas, me stay watch for bad men. Send Tomas if see bad men. BJ tell General Peso good want live in peace."

"Don't worry Peso I will make him understand."

As Josie and me rode on over the rise she rode in close to me and took my hand in her soft small hand and we stopped for a moment and she looked in my eyes to say.

"I feel like I belong here close at your side. I just hope that me being the daughter and niece of two evil men that has crossed paths with your family will not stop what I feel for you or what you might feel for me."

I could not believe what I was hearing coming out of the beautiful full red lipped mouth as I looked deep into the beautiful woman's dark blue eyes with that dark red hair flowing down to her thin well shaped waist that rode next to me.

9

The sentry stopped us as we came within a mile of the General's camp. "Who goes there? State your business?"

"I'm BJ Taylor and this is Josie Walters and we're here to see General Cook on behalf of my father Silver Buck Taylor."

A Sergeant came out of a small tent and looked at us then came over along with another corporal.

"I heard and this is the son of the man the General has been waiting for. Corporal Dean ride as fast as you can and wake the General and I'll escort Mr. Taylor and his young lady into camp."

Corporal Dean took a flying leap into his saddle and his horse was gone. Then I said to the sergeant.

"There are two men up on that ridge." I pointed the ridge out to the sergeant and the sentry. "They are my men and one is an Indian but he's a friend and the other is a Mexican with a drooping mustache. If they come riding in fast it means the Comancheros are coming." The Sergeant said as he jumped in his saddle.

"Sternberg, you heard what Mr. Taylor said so stay alert and if either one of his men come riding in fast you bring them to the General's quarters and fast."

The Sergeant lead the way and when we arrived at General Cook's tent he was standing outside fully dress in his military uniform with his saber at his side and his big, brimmed cavalry campaign hat on shading his eyes from the rising sun. The Sergeant dismounted fast and stood in front of the General and saluted and the General said.

"At ease Sergeant Muldoon."

Josie and me came out of our saddles at the same time as the Sergeant and stood right behind him with our reins in our hands. Then the General called for Lieutenant Cavy. The Lieutenant was out of the General's tent as soon as he heard his name.

"Cavy, you'll want to hear this."

The Sergeant introduced Josie and me then he asked to be dismissed.

"You may be excused back to your post with Dean."

"Thank you Sir."

We watched as the two rode out to the sentry post.

"Mr. Taylor you and your lady please come into my quarters."

"General, I know you have your protocol but there might not be time for all this."

"I see, then please continue."

"It's a long story but here's the short of it. This is Miss Walter and her Uncle Jeb Martin is the leader of a band of Comancheros that has been selling guns to the Indians and my father Silver Buck and a small party blew up a barn and a train full of rifles to be sold to Chief San Juan and Chief Victorio and now they are on our trail less than a half days ride maybe less by now. My friends are up on the ridge watching for them. One is a Mescalero Apache that Victorio had tortured and left for dead and we saved him. He wanted peace with the white man so now he is helping us. They cut out his tongue and placed him on an anthill. I can interpret his signing if need be."

"Sir, I am Josie Walter's and I came to live with my uncle about two months ago after my aunt died. I did not know what kind of man he was then but now I know and have seen all his doings."

"Where is your father, Silver Buck?"

"He is coming this way with Foster, his partner and Peso's wife and son Juan. Victorio might be on our trail also."

"Peso, I've heard of him. I heard that he has wanted peace. Where is he? I would like to talk to him."

"Up on the ridge keeping watch for Martin's Comancheros."

"Lieutenant send someone for him and then get the troops ready to ride out."

"I better go with whoever you send cause he thinks that you may not trust him but he can lead you to Victorio village. We got his son out of that village about a month ago. Josie you stay here and rest. General if you can take care of her and her horse we have been through a bit of trouble."

"We will do that, son."

The Lieutenant was gone and back came another Corporal and we headed toward the ridge. As we left I saw the General lead Josie into his tent out of the now boiling noon sun and her horse was being led away and then I heard the bugles sound. The Sergeant rode along with us when we passed the sentry.

"Sergeant let me talk to Peso and I'll tell you what he says. He can hear but cannot speak. Victorio had his tongue cut out and left him on an anthill. So he don't trust many people."

"By God I wouldn't either."

I waved at Peso and Tomas as we came near. As we reached the ridge Peso was already signing.

"Blue coats soldiers, want me?"

I was telling the Sergeant all that Peso was saying as we talked.

"Yes, but not in a bad way. The General wants your help in finding Victorio and Martin."

Tomas spoke up.

"The General will get to meet Senor Martin soon you can see him coming."

Tomas pointed to the west and the Sergeant took his binoculars out and had a look for his self.

"He looks to have about hundred men behind him and I would say he's about three miles off." Then Sergeant Muldoon turned to Peso.

"Don't be afraid. We do need your help to guild us. But right now we have to hurry and get ready for what's coming. Who are they?"

"I was telling General Cook, that is the Comancheros lead by a white man named Jeb Martin."

Tomas put in. "He is a bad man."

"Then we have no time to waste."

The Sergeant turned and we followed his lead and as we neared the General was out in front of his command of about two hundred men and I saw there were another, I estimated three hundred left in camp. The Sergeant stopped in front of the General and saluted.

"Sir, the Comancheros that we have been looking for so long are right over that rise about three miles away."

"Good Sergeant, this must be Peso that I have heard so much about. I'm glad that you want peace with the white man now if you would be my scout for this campaign I would be much in your gratitude. Mr. Taylor, whom may this other gentlemen be that is with you?"

"This is Tomas who used to work with Martin but is tired of the way Martin is cruel to most everyone."

"Well, we can sure use you. Mr. Taylor if you and Tomas will assist Peso as scouts and assist my Colonels I would be in all your debt. Colonel Belsize if you will take Company B to the left flank just below the crest and take one of the new scouts but not Peso he's with me. Then Colonel Potter, you take your company to the right flank just below the crest. I'll take Company A with me up the center. Peso and your scouts will watch over the crest for when the Comancheros are within a hundred yards of you and let us know. Then on my command we'll attack and encircle them on all sides with only their rear left open."

"General, Peso can't talk only sign."

"I appreciate the thought but you had no way of knowing but I know sign. I've been fighting out here many years." The General was signing as he talked to me. Then I looked Peso's way and he was signing to the General.

"Like this white soldier of many bars. Get along good."

The General laughed out loud and signed back.

"I think so. Now, Mr. Taylor I left your lady in my tent to sleep."

"Thank you sir."

"Everyone to their positions and when Peso gives the sign we attack on my command. Take them alive if possible but fire if fired upon and I don't mean to wound."

The companies went to their positions and us scouts dismounted and climbed to the top of the rise and I could see Martin in the lead about a mile and half away looking like he had the world whipped. He didn't know what his future held in the next half hour. As I scanned the area north and south of where Martin's men were I could barely make out four riders coming at a fast pace from the southwest. They looked as if they were trying to give Martin's Comancheros a wide berth. They looked as if they knew where they were heading as they came closer. Not anyone from Martin's bunch had seen them cause they were concentrating on what was ahead of them. About then I saw Peso give the sign and I looked and the Comancheros were nearly on top as the General gave the order to attack. Peso, Tomas and me were on our horses in a matter of seconds as the whole command when over the rise with the bugles sounding in our ears as they went by. As we made the rise there was already firing from all sides. I saw horses fall on top of men and men being shot out of their saddles as the soldiers closed in on all three sides. I saw the four riders had slowed their pace as they had saw the soldiers come up over that ridge and swarm all around Martin's men. This is when I recognized who the riders were. My Pa was in the lead and Foster behind him and Juan and Solie coming up behind. The General was off to the side with Peso by his side as most of the Comancheros had raised their hands with very few still fighting. As I rode over to talk to the General one of the Comancheros was dismounted and was about at Peso's back with a gun pointing point blank at the General. I whipped my whip off my shoulder and it went singing through the air and caught the gun and flung it in the air to land in front of the Generals horse and one more fling and my whip was around the man's body as I pulled him off his feet. I jumped off Red and had my rope in my hand as I dropped the handle of my whip and tied up the man. The General and Peso had turned as my whip had first flown through the air.

"Good going Mr. Taylor you are sure handy with that whip. I was wondering about it when I saw it wrapped around your shoulder."

"Comes in handy sometimes. I was coming to tell you if you look over this way." I pointed to the southwest. "You'll see my father coming with Peso family."

As they looked I could see a big smile come across Peso's face when he saw his family. As we were watching I saw Pa break off from the others and put Blacky to a full gallop and that is when I saw Martin break away from the fighting to the south at neck breaking speed.

The General and Peso were watching as I pointed Martin way.

"Don't worry General, Martin's as good as caught with Silver Buck on his tail."

"Looks to be the case look at him gaining on him."

Peso signed. "Family coming me go meet them."

"General, I'll go see if I can be of any help to Pa if you don't mind."

"You two go ahead this battle is about over. These Comancheros are no match for my soldiers. I'll watch this one that is hog tied on the ground until my commanders wrap this thing up. We'll talk later."

Peso and me headed in different directions with both of us in a hurry as I put Red to a full gallop it was clear that Pa didn't need any help as he had his lasso to full loop and flung it as Martin was firing back at him. Then the loop found its way through the air around the body of Martin as Martin was still trying to shoot from the saddle to the rear without any success so I gave Red a rest and slowed down. By the time I rode up he had Martin tied up and back in the saddle. I heard Martin telling pa.

"What is the meaning of this? We were just riding along to find Josie and find out why she left." I told Martin.

"You can discuss that with General Cook and I'm sure Josie will be there to tell you and the General why she left."

"Wait, just let me go and I'll be leaving. She can stay wherever she wants to be."

"Son, what are you two talking about?"

"Pa, it's a long story but I'm sure there are going to be parts you won't understand and others that I hope you will. Like the love of a beautiful woman."

"Now I'm really confused but I understand that last part."

"Let's get back to the Generals headquarters and you'll find out."

"We have news for the General and Peso."

As we rode back with Martin all tied up in front of us we saw Peso heading toward the encampment ahead of us. As we came into camp Peso was already standing in front of the General with Josie by his side. Buck jumped off Blacky and grabbed Peso with a hand on each shoulder.

"Good to see my friend again all well with my son."

Then BJ picked Josie up in the air and swirled her around.

"Good see friend Buck Taylor. Tell General what Solie told. Friend General Cook my people coming have two hundred warriors. Victorio leading them follow tracks. Two sunrises away from Peso and friends with lodges means women and children with them. Ask as friend; let Peso talk to Victorio and my people. Will tell you here. Many my people want peace as I do. They do not know Victorio had this done to me for talking peace." He stopped as he signed and pointed to his mouth and opened his mouth then pointed to the scars all over his body from the anthill. "Some will leave with me and my friend Buck Taylor has said we can live near this place in peace." The General said to Peso and Colonel Belsize.

"Take this all down word for word as I tell Peso Colonel Belsize."

"Yes sir." Then Colonel Belsize went into the tent and came out with a small desk and chair with paper and ink and a quail pen. He sat and was ready to write as the General spoke and signed at the same time.

"I speak the truth to my friend Peso. We do not want to hurt or kill your people. Some of both of our people have been cruel to each other. If you can get your people not to fight we can sit down and find an area of land that you and your people will want to live on always. But there are always people on both our side that will not want peace, like Martin and Victorio, they will do almost anything to keep this war going. My troops will not harm the women and children of the warriors that do not want peace. Only the warriors that fight and when we agree on land for your people I will put it in writing for future people to know what I have promised to you."

"Will start now to meet my people one day ride from here. Not come back two suns friend Cook will know Peso failed. Come to here and you know people with Peso are peaceful."

"I understand."

"Ask one thing my friend Buck Taylor, BJ please go with me." I spoke up.

"Your friend Buck Taylor will go with you. I'll let BJ answer for his self. After what you and he did BJ is now a man to speak for his self."

"Peso, I will be proud to go."

"Leave soon."

"Now son who is this girl and how did she get here?"

"You know that long story that I was telling you about well this is it."

I told pa the whole story as Josie stood by my side holding my hand. After I told pa everything I said.

"She is a Walters but she did save our lives and she was just a baby when you had trouble with her family a long time ago. When she found out what her uncle was doing she wanted to leave but had no other family to go to and she didn't know anyone out west. Her uncle told her the truth after she yelled at you across the river."

"I see, what do you have to say young lady."

"My aunt and me had no idea what her brother, my father, and her husband was up to. I just couldn't see BJ hurt or killed by Uncle Martin after I found out the truth. My aunt didn't bring me up that way."

"But you are a Walters. I guess I'll just have to deal with that part. You do seem nice and you seem to like my son."

"Yes sir, I do and I'm just two years older than him."

"You already figured that out have you?"

"We'll have to get to know each other when we get back."

"One more thing Pa her friend is with her and he was one of Martin's right-hand men but he helped Josie get us out of there and he helped in the capture of Martin's Comancheros and he does want to live in peace and be close to Josie and I promised him a job on the ranch."

"Well now that beats everything now you not only want me to take in the daughter of the murder of my great-great grandfather but also a Comanchero to work with me?"

"Pa, I know you have a big heart. I've seen it all my life and now I ask this favor of you as your first-born son. Here comes Tomas now. Tomas shake hand with my pa Silver Buck."

Tomas grabbed his hand and shook it like there would be no tomorrow with that big grin on his face.

"Senor, I have heard much about you. You came in among us and blew up all the guns and the big train. I didn't think anyone could do this kind of thing to senor Martin. You are a great man. It made me, want to leave and never come back."

Tomas quit shaking Pa's hand and started slapping him on the back all the time with that big smile still on his face under that big mustache.

"I can't say no to a speech like that and there are a few of your people in Durango. Tomas you should feel right at home as long as you have given up your bad ways."

"Si, Tomas has never killed anyone except to protect Tomas life. This is the truth senor Silver Buck."

"Alright, now we need to leave BJ or we're never going to get back home."

We ate a meal and Corporal Dean packed our saddlebags with food. Then I saw Peso with Solie and Juan. Foster came to see us as we ate.

"I'se am going to the ranch and let the folks know what's going on. We'se only twenty miles or so and I'se can make that on Lagger in one day."

"That is good of you Foster. I know Red Bird and the children will want to know we are so close to home. Tell Pa and Sam to have the men ready in case this doesn't happen the way we want it to. Don't tell Red Bird that we're in any danger. Only we are part of a peace committee that is trying to see peace come between the whites and the Mescalero Apaches. We hope to have no more killing on either side. Take Solie and Juan with you and also Josie, BJ's new friend with the pretty red hair and her protector Tomas and tell Red Bird to look after all of them and try to make them feel wanted."

"I'se tell her that but you'se know Red Bird better than I'se do. She will know deep down that you'se are trying to spare her worry. I'se know she will also take well care of Peso family. I'se was wondering who that pretty red head was. Looks about the right age for BJ." Then BJ spoke up.

"Now Foster she's just a friend and she is two years older than me."

Foster looked BJ square in the eyes and as he turned around to walk away he said.

"I'se saw that look in her eyes when she looked at you'se. Saw that same look in your ma's eyes when she first saw your pa." Foster disappeared from sight.

We three jumped on the back of our horses and started off to the land of the west that might hold many dangers for us. The General stopped us long enough to say.

"If at all possible send one of you back to let us know what happened so we can prepare."

"We'll try." Is all I said as we rode off to our unknown meeting.

As we rode to the west I knew that this time of year we would have no bad weather and the days would be bright and hot. Peso signed to us.

"Might meet one more sunrise from now. My friends stay back half a mile from main camp. Peso go talk if swarm all over Peso my friends head back to friend Cook and tell him."

"We want to go in with you."

"No, friends be in danger that far away. No need any closer Victorio have guards to watch two miles away."

We rode on toward the now setting sun. We rode on into the night just stopping long enough to let the horses rest and eat grass and oats we had brought and horses and men alike drank from the creek and as we sat and ate BJ asked as a friend.

"Tell me Peso what will you do when you ride up to Victorio. He will know you are not a ghost and had tried to make a fool out of him in front of his braves."

Peso was trying to laugh out loud but could not but there was a big smile on his face that showed his joy at the thought. Peso signed.

"Peso, not know. Try to talk to all people not let Victorio get me alone again. Is how got all this done to Peso. Try not to let happen again. Know Victorio be mad for reason BJ says."

We went on away from that nice little spot into the black of the night not knowing what we were riding to. Our deaths or peace for everyone but we would know the answer tomorrow night. Then the moon came up and we bedded down for a few hours' sleep and in the morning we would continue to keep on going to our fate. As we laid there with no fire burning and as I could hear the creek bumbling and the coyotes howling and that sound of the horses chomping on the grass knowing they were all right. I spoke to Peso.

"You know Peso the thought came to me that if you thought you could beat Victorio in a hand-to-hand fight and the winner could decide what would happen to your people, peace and survival or war and fight till no more Mescalero Apache's are left. Even the children would be gone."

Not any answer came my way as I drifted off into the darkness of sleep. A dream came to me in the night. I was seeing Red Bird's people and that loveable man known as Dancing Bear that was Chief and Red Bird's father. Now I was seeing what might have been if Dancing Bear had not been as intelligent as he was to break away from a warring tribe to start his own peaceable tribe. There might not had been a Red Bird and if there were she would have hated all white men and would not have come to me as my lovely wife and our four beautiful babies would have never lived on this earth to love and be loved. To grow into the man like BJ has become. I was still dreaming as I was shaken awake by BJ and the light of the dawn could be seen in the eastern sky as I opened my eyes and smelled breakfast cooking on a very small fire with no smoke rising into the dawn.

"Pa, you were asleep like a log. That was the third time I've shaken you."

"I was having a dream about your mother and our babies."

"Even me."

"Yes son even you. No matter how much of a man you become you will always be your mothers and my baby to always be loved. Where's Peso?"

"He's got the horses ready to go and is up on the ridge scouting ahead. You know Peso always ready for anything."

Peso came in off the ridge that was engulfed fully in the brightening of dawn and we ate our small breakfast without much being said till Peso let us know as he signed.

"Thinking in a dream and what Buck Taylor say last night. One way to stop Victorio and dream powerful when comes before battle. Today Peso think what more can do."

"So you did hear me. I had me a dream also and think your people will survive this and live at peace for many years alongside the whites and one day my and your children's children will get along and your people with help my people in some great way. I think our God has planned all of this to make both our people realize we need each other." BJ put into the conversation.

"I know Juan and me get along great and we have a lot in common. Maybe cause Grandfather Dancing Bear taught me a lot of the ways of his people and mother never stops teaching us as we grow up."

The sun was starting to stick its fiery self above the horizon as we rode on with the sun's rays at our back warming up the day. At noon we stopped alongside a brook that ran south from under the boulders of the area that we had come into now that we were further west. Peso signed which he hadn't done all day, as I knew he was thinking about what he could do when we reached Victorio village.

"Thoughts not come to Peso."

"The thoughts will come as we ride cause I know you are right. Just look at the way our two families have become true friends. Don't worry about your family Foster took them to our ranch and Red Bird will take good care of them and Juan will have a great time with my younger children." Peso signed back.

"Yes, think we should be friendly to the white man. Never thought one would save life. The rest of Buck Taylor family like you my family alright if not come back."

Peso rode ahead of us a good two miles, as we were getting closer. We could see him on every ridge that we came to searching the area ahead. Then mid-afternoon Peso came riding up to us all excited and signed.

"Village over next rise and look." Peso pointed to the east behind us and as he turned he pointed to the north and then south as we stopped.

"Watch us see what we do. Know no one else with us for have been watching long. Sent two braves to where sun and moon come up."

"What happens now?"

"Buck Taylor, BJ come with Peso to top of ridge. Let my people know Buck Taylor not hide to cause harm only here to watch. Pesos go to village after BJ and Buck Taylor on top of ridge. No matter what happens do not touch guns they will kill. If Peso is killed try get away to friend Cook. Lookout will kill if can."

We three rode to the top of the ridge and there in front of our eyes were at least two hundred teepees. Peso signed.

"Many warriors Peso needs to take as many braves and family away so rest will see peace is only way for our people to survive."

As we sat there Peso rode off down the ridge toward the village by his self. As he came closer three-armed braves rode up to Peso and a look of amazement came over their faces as they rode into the village toward the lodge in the center of the village. Dogs were all around barking and children were running trying to keep up with the riders as their mothers tried to pull them back out from under the pony's hoofs. Peso is on his own now as he entered the village and he may get to tell us what happened later.

****

10

The village was as I had seen it before in many other places. The three braves rode with me to the center of the village where I knew Victorio's lodge would be. His lodge was always the largest in the village. There were running children all around us looking at me, then their mothers were running after their children trying to keep them from getting trampled by the ponies hoofs. The women would look at me in horror as they saw my scars from the anthill. Some braves spoke to me in our tongue and I would sign back as we rode slowly up to Victorio's lodge. The braves riding with me jumped off their ponies and went in the lodge but I stayed mounted for it is the custom of our people that a guess does not dismount till the Chief acknowledge one to do so and I felt that this was not my village any longer. I sat on my pony with my rifle across my legs in a not aggressive way so not to alarm anyone. It was long that I waited for Victorio to come out of his lodge with the whole village around could hear them talking about me.

"Is that Peso? What happened to him?"

"Must had been the white man that did this to him."

"Our people would not do this to their own kind." The talk continued all around and this was what I had wanted to be able to do speak to the braves and squaws. I was not expected to speak before the Chief came out and acknowledge me in front of the whole village but I could not wait for this to happen Victorio might not let me speak, so I started speaking in sign to my people that I had known all my life and now they looked at me like a stranger.

"I am Peso of this village and you all know me from a few moons ago. White men did not kill me as you have been told. It was white men that saved my life and they sit proudly up on that ridge looking down on us. They are brave men to go against what Victorio had order done to me."

I opened my mouth and the braves and squaws backed away from me a few steps in shock. "Yes, it is horrible what was done that is why I sign to you it is the only way I can speak. These scars are all over my body from being staked out on an anthill like our people have done to many of our enemies but I am not your enemy but this was also ordered done by your leader Victorio. I want the best for my people and know we can live in peace with the white man. The men that saved my life have become my great friends. I have also talked to the white man's great General and he does not want to harm you he just wants to live in peace with us. If you keep fighting he will fight and many of the braves will be killed and your squaws will mourn but less and less Mescalero's babies will be born as more and more braves are killed then in a few years our people will disappear from mother earth when it could all have been prevented."

Victorio stepped out of his lodge and raised his arms high in the air with a look of anger on his face. Then he spoke in the Mescalero language, part Spanish and part Apache.

"Why do you speak to my people before I am here in front of you?"

"To only tell them the truth about what you ordered done to me. This was not done by the white man as my people have been told to them. My son, Juan has told me what you have told to all our people. Yes, Juan is with his mother and me now. I came in your village one night and took him to his mother where he rightfully belongs not with Victorio as would have been to make a warrior to die for a loss cause."

"These are all lies that the white man makes him say to get my proud people to give up and live the way the white man wants us to live. Never to roam across mother earth as we have always done."

"Some of what Victorio say is true we would not be able to roam as far as we use to but that was only to follow the buffalo but now there are few left to hunt for their fur for winter. We have to find other ways to warm ourselves. The old ways are slowly dying. The white man can teach us the new ways but we can also keep many of our old beliefs that are in our minds that no one can take away from us. Victorio did this to me and if the braves are here that did this to me will speak. They will be afraid to speak for the same thing will happen to them. Victorio has not denied having this done to me."

"I, Victorio do deny this. It was the white man like I have told you, my people."

"Victorio lies to his people. Victorio is no leader in my eyes."

"Peso cannot come into Victorio village and say that I lie."

"I, Peso want to take my people with me to become their new leader to live on our own land among the white man and live in peace always. I challenge Victorio to fight me to end this and if I win whoever wants to can follow me and live in peace can do so without harm and the rest can fight till they are no more on mother earth."

"I Victorio will take up the challenge but as Chief I can appoint a great warrior to fight in my place for I am Chief and much older than Peso so I say Taka the great warrior in battles with whites will have the honor to fight Peso in my place."

"Peso agrees to Taka and Peso knows that Taka is great fighter. Once best friend and I think in my mind he still is."

"Fight will happen when the sun is half across the sky and knifes, tomahawks will be the only weapons to be used and I Victorio say if Peso wins whoever wants to leave can leave with Peso with no harm to come to them by Victorio or braves."

"Peso asks Victorio if friends on ridge can come into village to witness this fight and if I lose they will be let to go back to their people?"

"This will be done." Victorio pointed to the three braves that had rode in with Peso and they rode away to the ridge.

****

As three Indians neared we didn't know what was happening so I signed to them as they came right up to us.

"What does this mean?"

"Victoro will let you witness fight Peso have with Taka a great warrior in tribe has honor fight in place of Victorio."

They didn't ask for our guns as we rode into the village surrounded by many of Peso's people. Then we were in front of the war Chief Victorio as we were instructed to dismount and our horses were led away and we were placed in a teepee and there was Peso waiting.

"What does this mean, Peso?" Peso signed.

"Said wanted to come village."

"But are we prisoners?"

"No, just here to watch fight that will make it happen for people to leave if want to leave with me if Peso wins. If lose will be set free to return home."

"When is the fight?"

"When sun halfway across sky let know."

"If you lose you will go with us to our home and your family?"

"No, Peso's spirit will no longer be on earth. Buck Taylor must promise Peso to take care of family."

"I will but I know you will be going with us with many of your people."

"Knives are sharp and tomahawks very deadly." This is all Peso said as we waited for the fight with knifes.

We waited for the sun to rise to the noon of the day as Peso prepared his self for the fight to come. He had no knife or tomahawk these would come when the fight started but Peso sat with his legs cross and his arms to the sky in prayer. I knew some of what Peso was praying in his silence for I have seen Dancing Bears people do some similar prayers. The time was near now we knew when two braves came in to take us to where the fight would take place.

We were taken to the center of the village where a large circle was with a large fire built in the center of the circle. Braves were all around the circle but no squaws or children were to be seen anywhere. As we came up to one side of the circle Taka was on the opposite side with the fire in the middle. Taka had painted his face and upper body black with yellow stripes up and down his face and white stripes on his body. Peso had done none of this. Peso signed to us as we stood watching what was going to happen.

"Circle of braves so we cannot run away. Taka or Peso run out circle will be killed by one of braves."

"Peso, when I told you to fight I didn't know it was to the death. This is very serious."

"Know Buck Taylor did not know this but Peso know. Only way set my people free live life in peace."

One brave came to Peso and another went to Taka to hand them a knife and tomahawk. All around us the rest of the braves were yelling and chanting as Peso moved to the right and Taka moved to the left around the fire. They both had the knife in one hand and the tomahawk in the other as Taka rushed in at Peso with a snarl on his face and took a swing at Peso with his tomahawk but it swung wide as Peso ducked under it and came up with the knife which grazed Taka across his upper arm. Taka backed off and Peso looked cool and calm as he rushed toward Taka with the tomahawk raised but it didn't come down as Taka backed away. They moved around the fire to look each other in the eyes. Their feet were moving through the dirt at a fast pace now when Taka raised the tomahawk and came down toward Peso head but Peso caught Taka's wrist before it hit him and Taka tried to come up with the knife in the opposite hand to slice Peso across the belly but Peso caught that wrist also. As Peso had ahold of both of Taka wrist Peso leaned back to fall in the dirt on his back but he didn't let go of Taka wrist and brought Taka with him to the ground then as they hit the ground Peso put both feet into Taka belly and kicked him over his head to hit hard on his back. Peso jumped up and picked up his knife and tomahawk where he had dropped them and turned to see Taka laying in the dirt getting up slow as Peso rush him with the tomahawk raised and came down to slice Taka into his shoulder which made Taka drop his tomahawk in the dirt. The blood was flowing down Taka's arm mixing with the colors and dripping off the end of his fingertips into the dirt. That arm was hanging to Taka's side useless now in the fight but he had the knife to fight with. Taka kept trying to reach down in the dirt for the tomahawk instead of the knife but every time he did this Peso would rush him and take a swing at Taka and Taka would back away from the tomahawk. Peso finally kicked the tomahawk into the fire, which would make it too hot to handle and burn up the wood handle leaving only the steel that was useless without the handle. Taka moved round the fire and came at Peso with the knife raised to come down into Peso thigh and Taka held on to the knife and it came out but this left Peso limping on his right leg around the fire with blood rushing down his leg onto his foot. Then the blood was mixing with the dirt and made mud that clung to Peso foot. Peso was bending over looking at his wound and Taka rushed Peso with his knife raised high and started to come down when Peso brought his knife up to go all the way into Taka's belly not to come out. Peso knife was still sticking in Taka as he fell in the dirt on his face not to get up again. Four braves rushed in to carry Taka to his lodge as Peso limp over to us dragging his leg through the dirt. BJ and me rushed in to grab Peso under each arm and help him to the lodge we were in before. Two squaws brought a wood bowl with water and soft deerskins. Peso lay there as we cleaned his wound.

"You won Peso."

"Lose friend Taka, we friends since little boys. Did not want to harm Taka. Had to for my people."

The flap of the lodge came open and Victorio came in and stood looking at Peso a long time.

"Victorio ordered Peso tongue be cut out and put on anthill to die. Victorio thought Peso afraid of white man always talking of peace. Victorio see now this is not true. Not run like Victorio thought Peso would. Taka will live knife through side. Taka long time get well. Victorio think now, let Peso know what decides." Victorio turned and walked out.

"What does he mean he'll think about what to do?" Peso signed.

"Peso, not know. Peso know Victorio not always keep word. Wait, see Peso need time to get strong again."

Food and water was brought to us as we waited all through the night. Peso slept most of that time. His leg had stopped bleeding and still looked good no infection as of yet and no fever. I saw BJ open the flap of the lodge once during the night and two braves were there with spears crossed to block him from leaving. I know I fell asleep sometime during the night but didn't know about BJ as I knew he wanted to be out of here as I did but I have more patience than him.

******

Foster was going to be heading north to the ranch with four new people that Silver Buck's family knew nothing about. They also didn't know we were so close. The ranch is so large sometimes the boys don't get to the south but once or twice a month especially in the dry summer months when the runoff from the mountains dry up in the southern part of the rivers. The cattle tend to stay away from this dry part of the ranch cause they water at the tanks that Buck had built that first year he bought the ranch. As we'se said good-by to General Cook to head north we'se still didn't know what was going to happen with Victorio. The Comancheros that were left were rounded up along with Martin and taken to Fort Collin's in the northern part of Colorado to stand trial in the civilian part of the town that now surrounded the Fort. With five of us it took longer than was thought but the next morning we'se spotted some of the ranch hands as we ate breakfast that Solie was still cooking. It was Sam in the lead.

"I'se be, what is the big boss doing out this far from the main house."

"Kind of thought we'd take a look see down south of the ranch. Thought we might spot Silver coming this way. You know Foster y'all been gone a long piece of time."

"What we'se had to do was important and I'se just bet Red Bird put you'se up to this."

"You know Red Bird and how she worries about Silver."

"Sam, you'se and the boys light and eat some great food that Solie made."

"Well, we'll light since there's no use going any further. You will know everything and we know how you like to tell stories. Now, Foster who are these new people I see in front of me." Sam said this as him and the boys were getting out of their saddles.

"We'll have some coffee ma'am but the boys ate at the bunkhouse and I ate at home what Ann is still fixing me every morning before she leaves for the store." He said this to Solie with his hat in his hands.

"Sam, I can speak for myself that grub looks good enough to eat."

"Pete you would say that. You would eat ten times a day if Juan cooked it. Sometimes I think you eat more in a month than we pay you." Foster started to tell his story.

"This is Solie, she is the wife of Peso that is with Silver and BJ south of here, about a day's ride. They'se with General Cook trying to make peace with Victorio."

As Foster talked Solie was off to the side by the fire holding Juan very close to her not knowing about these new white men with their guns. Then Foster continued as Sam had his coffee and Pete with some of the boys ate their second breakfast.

"The young man with Solie is Juan. He is the son of Peso and Solie."

Pete spoke up as Josie came closer to the circle of men.

"Foster, who is this red head."

"You'se going to have to ask BJ about her but since he's not here. This here is Josie. We'se found along the trail." Foster left her last name off for good reason he wanted to talk to Red Bird first and Sam knew about her father very well.

"What else happened out there?" Sam said.

"Sam, come up to the house later and we'se talk after I'se tell Red Bird everything."

"Sure thing Foster. I'll be there and bring Ross and Molly and may find out who that Mexican is."

Sam and the boys mounted and rode off to the ranch as we packed up everything and headed that way ourselves. We all five rode side by side and Solie said in her broken English.

"See now, use to Foster, Buck Taylor and BJ but white men with guns scare me."

"Solie, I'se know but guns are to protect the ranch and people from all harm. Sometimes even white men are bad but all white men are not. The same as with you'se people."

The ranch house came into sight as we rode we could see Red Bird on the front porch and Song Bird and the twins came running toward us as we rode up to the house as the sun rose up high in the sky. The word had reached the house already. First thing after I'se got off Lagger Song Bird had her arms around my neck.

"Uncle Foster you're back. Where's Pa?"

"He'se back a ways. He'se be coming soon."

Then the twin's jump in my arms as I'se reached down for them.

"Hi, Uncle Foster." They both said at the same time.

"You'se two are growing like weeds. You'se too big for old uncle Foster to pick up anymore."

Red Bird came down the steps and hugged me like I'se was a long-lost grandpa. Then she looked at the others.

"Foster, you left with Buck and my son BJ and come back with these new people. Please come up on the cool porch out of the blazing sun."

"Red Bird, it is a long story and Buck can do better telling of it than I'se can but this is Solie and her and Peso son Juan. Peso is with Buck, BJ and General Cook trying to bring peace to all for good. Buck is only two days away from the ranch but the General is counting on him and Peso." As Red Bird took Solie hands in her hands Foster said.

"They are Mescalero Apache." A look came into Red Birds eye that I'se had never seen before. Then Red Bird said in her now near perfect English after twenty years living in the white man's world and with a teacher like Jenny Gills.

"Welcome to you and your son to our house."

"Your man Buck Taylor say Red Bird make Solie and Juan feel at home."

"I will do my best. How are you Juan?"

"Me don't know, everything strange but father say we come to live in peace with white man and have to get use to different ways."

"Your father sounds very smart and brave to come into a new world like I did twenty years ago."

"Buck Taylor tell Solie and Peso about you and father Dancing Bear. Says friendly to all people if good and we good." Solie said this to Red Bird as Josie came up beside us.

"Now you'se may have to sit down before you meet Josie."

"Why is that young lady?"

"I think Foster means because of my last name." As Red Bird sat down on the swing in the shade of the porch Josie continued.

"It's Josie Walters."

For the second time that anger came into Red Birds eyes but as I'se talked the anger went away and the sweet Red Bird came back as nice as ever as Josie said.

"I was only two when Buck had his trouble with my family. I was sent to my aunt's when my mother died and had never known my father or even my brother and sister. When I came to live with my uncle Jeb out here after my aunt died my uncle filled me with hate for Buck but I didn't like what my uncle was doing, selling guns to the Indians. Then uncle told me the truth after I met BJ I knew that he couldn't have a father that was a murderer. I helped BJ and Peso escape from my uncle's Comancheros. That is the short of it and here I am."

"So you have met my son." Red Bird's other three children heard and were giggling. They knew what their mother meant. Red Bird heard them and said.

"You three go on outside for now. Hurry now and don't get underfoot of grandpa."

"Yes ma." The children said as Red Bird turned back to Josie.

"Yes ma'am. I got to know BJ some on the trail.

"Red Bird, I'se forgot one this is Tomas. Tomas I'se do not know you'se last name."

"I'm known as Tomas only. Never know my mother or father. I was raised by the padres of a little church 'til I was taken by some renegades and raised to be what I was 'til Josie came in my world and I saw how wonderful the world could be."

"What were you Tomas?"

"Tomas was one of Josie's uncle's Comancheros. I am not anymore. Senor Buck says there are many people of my kind in Durango. I just want to be normal and be close to Josie to help her if she needs my help."

Josie went to Tomas and put her arm around his shoulder as Tomas stood there with his hat in his hands and his head bowed.

"Tomas you know I'll always need your help."

Red Bird stood there in her own way of being honest with her hands on her still beautiful waist and said with true feeling.

"Foster, you know how I always speak the truth. You know how I feel about Apaches after what Geronimo's warriors did to my village and to Caroline and her mother. Then there's Josie after what your family did to Buck's great-grand-father. Tomas, my people never had dealings with your kind of Comancheros but I heard they were bad."

"I'se know you'se and the way you think since you'se were a little girl. I'se know you'se are kind and always treat people good if they are good and you'se forgive the ones that are not."

"Yes Foster, you are right. My husband is a very smart man and can see the truth inside a person's heart as he has learned from me after being married for these twenty years and if he knows that you are good people I also have a good feeling about you four inside my heart. So you can live in our home and we will see what happens. I can't wait to meet your husband Peso. I know I'll like him."

A big smile and relieve came to the faces of everyone as Red Bird went in close to hug everyone, yes even Tomas and then she said to her true friend Foster.

"You know me Foster after that hug all of you have been on the trail to long. Foster get to your house and Juanita will run you a bath."

"Oh, Red Bird."

"Go now, we have two water closets in this house and we'll use them both. Juan, I know you are frighten but you will be all right with Tomas for you both need a bath. You ladies can come to my room."

"Saw river coming here not too far. Know son and me not clean go to river get clean." Solie told Red Bird.

"That is all right I was the same way when I came to this house so you and Juan go down there and no one will bother you and then come back and eat."

"Solie fix food for Juan by river. General gave food to us for ride here."

"That will be fine Solie and if I can help you in any way come to see me or Tomas."

So Foster went out the door with Solie and Juan and I looked at Tomas.

"Tomas if you will feel better go on down to the bunkhouse and get clean up there. The men are on the range and only Juan the cook is there. Tell him I sent you and he'll feed you and get you a tub."

"Sounds to be one of my people."

"Yes he is. He can tell you about the town and the ranch in your own language."

Tomas left for the bunkhouse as Red Bird turned to Josie and looked her in the eyes.

"I don't think I'll have a problem with you leaving."

"Not me I've been wanting a real bath for weeks. Just lead the way to that tub and I'll be happy."

"I'll show you my water closet because everything a women will need is in there and I'll get Manual to fix you a great meal. You must be tired of that trail food."

"It wasn't bad Solie is a great cook."

"After we will have to talk more about you and my son."

"That would also make me happy to get to know BJ's mother and more about BJ."

"You will, I promise you."

Before Foster went to his house he went to Ross's house and Ross welcomed him in with a big handshake and a smile on his face. Then they heard a horse ride up and Sam came in.

"Thought you can tell us more about what's going on out there."

Ross looked at Foster.

"Bucks alright, ain't he?"

"This is why we'se come in early. Buck told me to tell you two and no one else not even Red Bird. He wants you'se to get the men ready for a war in case Victorio wipes out the General and his five hundred solders."

"Let's have the whole snoop now."

"When I'se left everything was fine for now. The Comancheros were all rounded up and Peso wanted to talk to Victorio and the General let him go and when we'se left Buck and BJ were leaving with him." This Foster said looking straight into their faces.

"To meet Victorio!"

******

11

I was restless all night long. The same dream kept coming into my mind over and over as I somewhat slept. I was way out on the desert all alone and a mirage was always in front of me about a half mile out in the desert. The mirage was a lush place of palm trees and huge oaks with willows beside the small lake that glimmered in the sun. There in the middle of the lake was my lovely wife Red Bird lying on a giant lily pad that floated on the top of the shimmering clear water and she was looking down into the water of the lake to look on her beautiful face. As I got closer I could see she was wearing nothing and was dipping her hand in the cool water and dripping it all over her lovely body. That is when I saw her calling me to come near with a jester of her fore finger bending in her direction but as I got closer and closer the sand of the desert got deeper and deeper till all my body was covered except my head as I was near the lake's edge. I heard her clear "Come to me my darling husband to my lily pad and you will be safe." This dream came back over and over during the, what seemed a long night.

Then someone was shaking me awake as the morning food and water were brought in and Peso was awake and sitting up already eating the food down and Peso signed.

"Peso good, hungry. Leg not hurt only some."

Peso tried to get the squaw to tell us what was happening but her mouth was shut tight and would not say a word. Peso signed.

"Buck Taylor not worry squaws not talk serving men. This went on for two more days and nights then the next morning a brave came in the lodge.

"Victorio decide you three come follow me."

As Peso tried to rise his self I could see the sign of a little pain from his leg wound so BJ and me went over and grabbed under each of his arms and lifted him to his feet then Peso looked normal as we walked to the flap that was being held open by the brave that came to get us. We saw out in front of the lodge there were people all around and very quiet as Victorio began to speak. This is when BJ jabbed me in the side and I looked out a ways from the circle of the lodges. There were not as many as before the fight. The lodges had been taken down and were on travois behind ponies. The number was around maybe ninety as I counted. Then Victorio spoke.

"Peso fight a brave fight against a strong warrior and had won. My people heard me give my word to Peso that my people would decide to go with Peso to so called peace with the white man or stay here with their Chief Victorio. My people have decided the last three suns that as many as the sunrises between three full moons and another are to go with a new warrior and soon to be new Chief of his own tribe Peso. They tell Victorio they are tired of war and the loss of many good braves. Some are not and they will stay with Victorio till we are all gone from Mother earth. This I say in front of all my people to be repeated by your young from now on. So go now as I watch with a tear in my eye." Victorio turned his back and went into his lodge.

Peso stood proud and strong as BJ and me mounted up on our horses that had been tied in front of the lodge and headed to the northwest. Peso stood as everyone passed him that was going quiet and strong till a travois came by with Taka on it still recovering from his wounds and Peso grabbed Taka's shoulder and shook it and smiled then we saw him sign to Taka as BJ and me was turned in our saddles and watched to read what Peso said.

"Peso glad did not kill good friend Taka. Taka now gets well to hunt the hills again. Happy Taka come with us."

Then Peso rode pass everyone that was leaving Victorio and took his place beside us. This went on as we headed toward our ranch and to General Cook that was waiting. That night was a sight to be seen by a white man I bet for the first time after all the lodges were erected around a large lodge in the center. Not a soul entered the large lodge and then after the sun started to go down BJ and me heard drums start to sound outside the lodge we were provided so we went out to see what was going on.

The sight before us was spectacular. The squaws had brought wood from I don't know where for we were still in the semi-desert but there it was a large, I should say very large fire lighting up the dusk. Two braves took us to a circle of braves that were sitting cross-legged around the fire. The circle was completed as BJ and me sat down like the others. We could hear drums being beaten as we saw braves rise and do dances similar to the ones performed by Dancing Bears braves at Red Birds and my wedding. As the night became darker and the full moon started to rise in the night skies the squaws brought food for everyone as a brave enter the circle.

"All know me but for our new friends I am Paka, brother of Taka. I speak for Taka who is over there lying wounded by a great warrior among our people. He is leading us to a great new peace alongside our new white friends. It took a lot of trust for us to leave Victorio but it is time we learn a different way to live in peace to raise our children in peace so there will be many more of our people in the future. Now we take a show of hands to have a new Chief to led us into this new way of peace."

Another brave stood up to speak.

"Manuel votes for Peso." Then he sat down. This went on as we ate till all ninety lodges had voted. Some lodges had single brave and other lodges had married braves then other were married with children. But each lodge had one vote and each one had been for Peso with no reservation. Even Taka was carried out to vote. Then Paka brought Peso to the center and placed a beautiful headdress on Peso head as he had been chosen as Chief. Then the new Chief signed.

"You will never hear my voice again but I give it up willingly for the peace that is to come to this village. Peso will not run this village alone. I will appoint braves that know the way of our people and we will decide things that happen together. Peso so wishes Solis and my brave son could be here now and be proud of Peso but my friends Buck Taylor and his great son are here to see this happen. Now I would ask my friend BJ to show all how uses whip. This done to show we except some white man's ways."

A look of amazement came over BJ's face as he stood and took his whip from his shoulder, BJ had not expected this but he was up for it and came in the center of the circle with the bright fire behind him his whip started to pop as BJ snapped it in the air over everyone's head. Then he spoke in sign for he knew many around us did not know English.

"Now I will show you how dangerous this bullwhip can be in a fight. This time no one will be hurt but it can hurt if someone does not know how to use it right." He let it whip through the air and into the fire which caused sparks from the fire to rise into the night sky like the 4th of July as a burning log came flying out of the center of the fire collapsing the fire down a foot. The burning log had landed, after flying through the air on the end of the whip to land at the feet of Peso the new Chief. This startled most everyone but not Peso he just sat there with arms crossed and a smile on his face. Then whipped the burning log up in the air once more over my head to come down right beside me and as fast as it landed BJ whipped it back through the air into the fire once again. This all took place in a minute or so. Then BJ brought Paka to the center of the circle and signed.

"Paka stand here and not move at all for this is very dangerous if you move." BJ reached down and picked up a six-inch twig off the ground and said to Paka.

"Open your mouth and hold this twig between your teeth and remember not to move. I know you are a very brave warrior."

Everyone was waiting to see what would happen to Paka as he stood there. Paka could only stand there after BJ said how brave he was. BJ stepped back about fifteen paces and turned toward Paka fast and without waiting but a moment let the whip fly through the air toward Paka and I could see that Paka eyes were closed tight and he did look nervous as the whip pop close to his mouth and the twig disappeared, all except a small inch of the twig between his teeth and lips. The drums pounded and the smiles were all around as Paka walked around the inner circle holding the small twig that was left to show to all the braves with a big smile on his face and sweat on his forehead. Then BJ signed again.

"This is a time for peace but in a fight to protect oneself this bullwhip can be deadly and a good weapon." BJ came and sat down after wrapping the whip around his shoulder again. Peso got up and sign.

"Leave morning to meet with General Cook. Do not be afraid as we come near blue coats. They will not fire on us. General has promised this. Peso leaves you to make camp; Peso with friend Buck Taylor and BJ go talk to General. After we have council to decide what to do what General tell us. Buck Taylor will speak for us, as Peso will. Peso trust Buck Taylor."

The next day we traveled through the heat with cloudless skies above the whole tribe. They saw this as a good sign for their people as we came within sight of the army and heard bugles sound through the air toward us. We seemed to be about two miles away when I saw three solders coming our way mounted and as they got closer Peso smiled as he saw General Cook in the lead. Then there were Colonel Potter and Sergeant Muldoon with him. They stopped within one hundred yards from us and the General raised his hand in peace and we rode out to meet them. As we stopped in front of them I started.

"Hello General, we were going to ride in to talk to you later."

"I couldn't wait to see for myself what was coming our way. This is a pleasant site to behold. How many are with you Peso?" Peso signed.

"Ninety lodges. Ninety braves with squaws and children. Two hundred new tribe, tribe break away from Victorio." I spoke as the General sat his horse and looked around in amazement.

"General, Peso was elected Chief of this tribe last night."

"Really, Peso I didn't give you much of a chance of doing much good but you must be very powerful among your people." As we were talking the squaws were setting up the village to be left here till they knew where their new home would be. The general continued.

"We will talk and we both will decide where you will stay in peace and how far your range will be. I just want you to think. Some whites will not like this and we cannot protect you always. You can keep your weapons and you have the right to protect yourself with the large area we will decide on as long as you do not make war on anyone outside your range."

"My people want peace and will decide council. Council will decide everything for people. Victorio still make war on whites. Peso people not blame for what Victorio does."

"Will you tell us where Victorio is when you left him? I know you are at peace with whites there are many whites and I cannot speak for what some might say or do but I will make it clear to all that you are peaceful and want to live in peace. We go now."

"Come to village when sun move behind mountain. Eat and friend Cook invited talk before council. Buck Taylor there to tell my people if Peso no understand."

As General Cook was about to leave Sergeant Muldoon rode up to us and saluted the General. The General saluted back.

"Sir,"

"What is it Muldoon?"

"Sir, a group of citizens rode up to camp. They want to know where Buck Taylor is."

"Well, did you tell them? How many are there?"

"Yes sir. But I didn't know whether to let them come over here. There are about ten men and three women, one Indian that looks to be Ute and the other a Mescalero Apache and Josie Walters and a young boy that is also Mescalero and the white men are fully armed." I spoke to Muldoon.

"Is Foster with them and a gray-haired man."

"Yes sir."

"General that is my wife Red Bird and my father and some of my men and you know Foster. Peso, can my wife and father and men come into your village?" As Peso signed there was a dust cloud coming over the horizon.

"This be a true sign of peace to let a Ute and armed white men come to village. Solie, Peso wife and Juan with them so Peso, say yes." General Cook said to Muldoon.

"I see them coming. Muldoon let us go back to camp and let the peace begin. See you tonight Peso. I'll have some areas we can look at." They turned their horses and as they headed out they passed Red Bird and as she rode Lagger up she dismounted and threw her arms around my neck and kissed me like there was no tomorrow.

Solie and Juan came and stood by Peso as Red Bird let me loose and I shook Pa's hand and then Sam's then patted Foster on the shoulder. "Hello old friend." Then Pa said.

"Good to have you home son. You can tell by your wife reaction you were surly missed." He laughed along with the rest of our men.

Red Bird turned a little red as I turned to Peso with Red Bird hanging onto my neck.

"Peso, this is my wife Red Bird and this is my father Ross then this here is Sam our foreman of our ranch." As Peso signed BJ stepped up and Red Bird hugged him and then BJ told everyone what Peso was saying as BJ looked over at Josie then I saw Red Birds reaction.

"Buck Taylor, wife is Ute but acts like white woman." This made Red Bird blush again as Peso continued. "Welcome to my village. Are welcome for meeting after sun goes down." I looked at Solie and said.

"Peso, won't tell you, Solie but I will. Your husband is the big Chief of the tribe." Solie looked at Peso.

"Knew many moons ago as our son was being born that Peso was great man now many more will also know that he is great and will be great leader."

As the day went on Red Bird and me walked through the village hand in hand and the men were given food and water and they found a nice spot beside the creek, that ran below the ranch, which Peso had led his people to. Then Red Bird turned to me and said as we saw BJ and Josie walking next to each other going out a ways to be alone but the loyal Tomas was there a ways back to see no harm came to Josie.

"Buck Taylor." I knew I must be in trouble when my wife starts a sentence like that. "That woman has eyes for our son and I see BJ looks at her the same way but right now I think that looks to be a nice cool creek over there and that's some big boulders it runs around. I think you need to take a bath for tonight's meeting and I always like the cool feel of the water on my body."

"Red Bird, you are the same spontaneous girl I married many moons ago. You know Josie is a nice girl she was just misled for a while. Now let's go my lovely wife."

"I take that for a yes."

We were gone two hours and we came back refreshed after the long absents from each other and as we came back to the village the sun was beginning to disappear and give way to the night. There we saw the General and his Colonel's along with Sergeant Muldoon as they came riding into the village. The center of the village was large with the large fire as before. Solie came up beside Red Bird and me and looked at us.

"Red Bird, I think Solie wants you to go with her. It's the custom of theirs that only men can attend the meeting like your fathers people."

"Yes, I have been with the whites to long I need to remember my peoples ways. Solie led the way."

As Red Bird left I saw Taka walking toward the General with Peso and as I walked up Peso told General Cook in sign.

"This is Taka, Taka is next to be Chief if Peso gone." Peso pointed to three more braves on each side of him. "Paka, Taka brother will be head of what Paka calls reservation patrol. Paka and his braves of as many fingers on two hands patrol all reservation land keep peace and protect. Manuel and Alberto will be on council. Eat now then talk future. People of village hear what we say will know with own ears what speak." The braves from the village were all around the outer circle with the women of the village behind them.

It was time to eat so the squaws brought the food for all and the meeting began as Peso rose and was the first to speak in sign.

"Peso new Chief, need help so council to help Peso. Friend General Cook council talk when General leave when sun high in sky. Buck Taylor here to help tell where Buck Taylor land ends. Is where Mescalero's Apaches land begins way to old land where hot always whites call Mexico and to where sun sets in great canyon to where sun comes up what whites call New Mexico. This Mescalero new land and now General Cook speak."

"Thank you Peso, you have a great idea about the Indian patrol. Any whites that come on reservation without permission and be held by your police for the army to deal with. You have to lock them up until we deal with them. This should keep more white men out. I know you need a large area to supply the food needs for the people you have and half of this area is very dry. Buck tells me you know where the water is hidden even in the dry land and this is where you have always lived. I am sorry for the white man killing all the buffalo but no one thought they would ever all die. There were so many. The land that you have told me where your people want to live is good for them and I will write this in white man's words for all Chiefs of our people to know in the future that this is your land for always as long as the peace is kept. I have talked to Buck and his father and Sam and the government will buy from the Taylor Ranch twenty head of cattle a month or as you know as one moon. These cattle will be given to your people for food when times are bad and the game is scarce around your area. Now we can sign these papers and this will be done. Buck can read the papers for you because you trust him to tell you the truth. Colonel Potter has written down every word you and I have said. These papers will always be in our big city Washington for everyone to read. Your council will have a copy to always keep. Add Colonel Potter that Peso and his braves may keep all their weapons as long as they use in peaceful ways and protection of his people."

"Good to have papers always. Indian children someday learn to read white man tongue. Can tell all people what signed in late sun." Peso signed.

Colonel Potter came forward with the papers when he was through with the second copy. I got up and read every word that was written.

"Peso, this is my word as a true friend of Peso's people. What I have said is what is written in the white man's words to always be held by Peso and his people."

The General sat down and signed the papers and then Peso signed with an X in place of his name.

General Cook was smiling and patting Peso on the back. Peso held up the two copies that he had signed for his people to see. Then he signed the second copy.

"Good Mescalero Apaches always place to live. Peso will talk to General Cook my friend with council." He signed.

The meeting broke up and General Cook and I were taken to Peso lodge with the council. We sat in a circle around a small fire and Peso started to sign.

"Friend General Cook council decided will tell where Victorio is when we left. Paka go with General to show. Not there Paka will track where Victorio go. Paka not fight Victorio with you only track."

"This is great news Peso we can use Paka and maybe one day some of your braves will scout for the army and get paid by the government. Money is like horses to your people. You can buy things at the trading post or Forts. Tomorrow morning we leave for I do not want Victorio giving Peso's peaceful people any trouble and maybe some of Victorio braves will leave him and come to your village." Then I turned to Peso and took his arm in mine.

"Peso, we will go home to ranch when General Cook leaves but I will be close by if you need any help. General if someone is needed to help Peso and his people get settle and handle their moneys I have someone in mind. Then some of my men and me can show Peso how to raise cattle so they will never go hungry."

"If Peso wants the help by all means. So now Peso I'll leave and get ready for tomorrow. Paka you can join us in the morning as we come by here. If we have permission to cross your land Peso." A smile came across Peso's face and he signed.

"Friend General, always welcome come on reservation in peace."

I went to our camp and Red Bird was standing there waiting for me along with everyone else.

"It is finished and now we go home tomorrow. We may have to come back and help Peso and his people learn to raise cattle. Red Bird one day I would like Dancing Bear and Peso to meet and maybe become friends."

"That may take some time but my husband can do almost anything. This I thought was impossible but you did it."

This night there was a clear sky and the full moon came out bright as we sat around the fire and talked about how the land was changing and the people right in front of our eyes as Sam played his guitar into the night. A few years ago we were at war with the Apaches led by Geronimo. As we sat there Red Bird said.

"Look at those two, it won't be too long until they will want to be together always." "You really think so. You know she is two years older or three."

"With love it does not matter."

"I know you're right most of the time."

"Only most." Red Bird let out a little giggle and we turn over and went to sleep in each other's arms. This was the first night Red Bird and me had slept in the same bed for all the months we had been separated and her body felt so good next to mine all night long.

We said our good-byes to Peso and his people as General Cook and his soldiers left led by Paka and two more braves. We headed north for home as the day grew bright with the morning sun. By noon we were on our ranch and on to the house as we passed all the cattle and watering ponds. We were all together once again even Foster was still with us after all these years.

12

The sight of the ranch house in the distant was all but amazing to my eyes. With Red Bird riding Lagger beside me and BJ and Josie coming up behind then I saw my mother on the porch coming down the steps with Song Bird beside her and the twins on the other side. As we rode up Song Bird and the twins broke away from ma and made a beeline to me as I got off Blacky.

"Pa, we were so worried about you." Song Bird said as she jumped into my arms and just about knocked me down.

"Little darling you've grown so much. I don't think that name fits anymore."

"Pa, no matter how big I get I'll always be your little darling."

"That's true but when those bees come around the honeysuckle it will sound funny calling you that. You are sixteen now."

"Oh, pa. They're just boys like BJ."

"That's where you're wrong your brother prove himself a man on this trip."

This is when the twins made it to my arms and I held both up high and they were giggling as I ticked them.

"Now Bob and you Summer." For she had taken to her middle name instead of "Indian" her real first name. Well, Robert just naturally became Bob. It was my father that first called him that and it stuck.

"Have you both been good and not got under grandma's feet to much?"

"They haven't son. You know I adore them both and Song Bird. They can't do much wrong in my eyes." Ma said this as she came up to me and hugged all three of us together. Then Pa walked toward us saying.

"Those three could run around our house forever and Molly would be in heaven. Now that BJ got his wings as a man we won't see him as much."

There was BJ and Josie getting dismounted when he heard his grandpa.

"Grandpa that's not true. I'll still love spending time with you and grandma."

"And Josie if I haven't missed my bet." Grandma said as she walked up and reached up for BJ neck to give him a big kiss on his now red cheek. Josie laughed as she hear this and saw BJ turn red.

"Oh, Grandma you have to embarrass me in front of everyone."

"That's what Grandma's are for when their grandchildren get to big for their britches."

Manuel came up and took Buck by the arm and squeezed tight.

"Senor Buck is good for you to be back. You have been missed as always. The town has been a buzz since they heard you were near. Now Manuel and Juan and Juanita has fixed everyone dinner in the bunkhouse so we all can eat and talk together once again as before."

"Let's go, it's time to eat."

As we walked in the bunkhouse all the men were there. Then I saw Josh with Carolyn and Ann must had come from her store and then I saw Bill with Jenny and they all had their children with them. All my dear close friends.

I went around hugging everyone and shaking hands of my friends that I hadn't seen in almost half a year. Bill came up and slapped me on the back and told me.

"Your old friend put this together after he showed up with Josie, Solie, Juan and Tomas. Can hardly believe that Walters had as nice a daughter as Josie and all she talked about is BJ."

"I was put back some when she was telling me off before she found out the truth. We are over that now. I can just see Red Bird's face when she heard who she was after her bother shooting me."

"How's the mine doing?"

"It's holding its own but nothing like it once was. Come in and we'll talk about it but the ranch is doing great with that railroad spur coming into Durango. You can get the cattle shipped out to where once you had to make that drive up north. Don't have to worry about outlaws trying to steal all the money and gold."

"I'll tell you Bill that cattle drive was hard, I thought at the time but that was child's play compared to what we just went through. I hope one day you'll meet Peso he is great and a very caring leader of this people. He can talk only sign cause Victorio had his tongue cut out and left him for dead on top of an anthill."

"We met his wife and boy. They were nice but very stand offish."

"They never have been around white people. The Mescalero's are used to the desert. Their new land starts south where my land stops. We will have to talk about the government buying cattle from me to feed Peso and his people since most of the buffalo are gone."

"Silver, you beat all. I thought you almost were killed and you still had time to make a cattle deal on the side."

We both laughed as we saw Tomas come up to us from across the bunkhouse. Tomas had his hat in his hands turning it around and around. His smile was wiped off his face when I said.

"Tomas, this is my best friend Bill Gills."

"Si senor we meet when first came to ranch. Good to see you again senor Bill. Tomas came from town I went to see some of my people that live in town."

"That is good Tomas but I know you there's something else bothering you."

Tomas nodded his head toward Bill.

"You can talk in front of Bill."

"Well, I want you to know Tomas is always honest with you after my bad ways when I was young. Like I said was in town and saw two of the old Martin men on the street tying up in front of the saloon. They were looking around at the people and Tomas knows they were looking at how the town is armed. Tomas does not know what this means but Buck should know."

"Bill, Martin was the head of the Comancheros that were selling rifles to the Mescalero's. We blow up all the rifles he had stored to sell to Victorio and Chief San Juan. General Cook rounded up Martin and most of his gang. A few must have gotten away. Right now General Cook is on his way to confront Victorio."

"You think John should know?"

"Maybe just to make sure any didn't escape the guards on the way to the fort."

"Come on Tomas you don't have to be afraid of John."

John was over talking to Josh and Carolyn when we walked up. I shook Josh's hand and hugged Carolyn and then I spoke to John as I shook his hand.

"John, Tomas here just told me that he saw two of Martin's men in town."

"I haven't met you Tomas. Good to meet you." John was saying as he shook Tomas hand then added.

"How would you know what Martin's men looked like." Tomas stood there not knowing what to say. Then I interrupted.

"Tomas was a scout for General Cook along with Peso and BJ and he remembers seeing these two. Right Tomas." Tomas was shaking his head yes with a big smile on his face again.

"Tomas remembers these two faces. They were right in front of me with guns in my face point blank. BJ came with his bullwhip and snapped the guns out of their hands right fast. Tomas will never forget those two faces or senor Martin's. They are very mean to all that does not do what they say."

"Tomas, you can go now we'll find out what's going on and let you know."

When Tomas was out of hearing John said.

"He was downright scared of me."

"You and the badge. He was part of Martin's gang but when Josie came he changed. Tomas helped Josie, BJ and Peso escape from Martin's camp and Josie stopped Martin from having BJ whipped with his own whip by Tomas. Tomas had always been afraid of Martin but Josie gave him the courage to leave with her. So don't let him know that I told you. I'd trust my live with him now."

"I know what Martin's men have done to towns south of here so that's a hard one to overlook. I trust your judgment. I won't bother Tomas. He came to us with this information. I better get to town and send off a few wires to the fort and towns around. Carolyn, Josie I'll be seeing you."

I turned back to Josh and Carolyn.

"I know you heard that but give Tomas a chance. He has changed and don't repeat what you heard about Martin. We don't need a panic on our hands."

Carolyn spoke up as Josh hugged her.

"After the hurt ma and me went through if one man can change maybe more will with more good women coming out here."

"More than one. I know it's hard for you to trust Indians but Peso and ninety braves have changed if the white men will give them a chance."

"It would be nice to meet him we met his wife and son." Josh said as they gathered up their now three children and left for their horse ranch.

Red Bird came to my side as all the children had gone outside and tried to ride Bobby's new bicycle with that big wheel on front that had just came out and he had to have one but Bobby had to get on it by leaning it by the porch and jumping on and peddle. For me I'll stick to Blacky for riding.

"What was all that talk about with John and Tomas and then John rode off for town."

"Not much for now. Tomas thought he saw two of Martin's men in town. John just wants to make sure that Martin and the rest of the Comancheros made it to the fort for trial. You know how John is."

"Tomas thought or he knew them."

"For now let's just say thought."

"Alright dear but I just got you home and the house is ours tonight. The children are spending the night with grandma and grandpa and BJ feels more comfortable in the bunkhouse for tonight. He said only for tonight."

"I think he knows what his ma has planned for his pa. For one I can't wait to see that bath tub with my wife in it."

"You know my dearest does need to clean up and he always needs my help."

Red Bird let out a giggle and we went outside to see everyone off as they went home or to work. For us we said goodnight to ma and pa and kissed the kids good-by and went up to our room. We didn't see Manuel. He was out of the way also and Josie was at Fosters house for the night and maybe more as a guess with plenty of room till she decided on what to do next.

It felt funny but great to sleep in my own bed next to my beautiful wife still full of energy after all these years. It was time to ride the range and see what was happening around the ranch. I headed for the bunkhouse where all the men were coming out and I saw Sam and waved to him and BJ as I walked up.

"Well, son you about ready to get back in your own bed after listening to all those snoring men last night."

"It wasn't any worst that listening to you out on the trail."

"He got you there Silver. I remember that from the cattle drive."

"I have to take that from my own son and now my ex-foreman."

I laughed at the expression on Sam's face.

"Don't look so worried Sam I was just kidding with you."

Sam looked at me and then turned to BJ.

"What you'd do with your pa out there in the desert? I never known him to have a sense of humor."

"Sam I put up with your humor all these years. Figured I needed some in my old age."

"You're not old pa."

Look who's talking now? The one that saved a damsel in distress and then came out with her liking him more than a lot."

"Oh, pa. You know we're just friends."

"Yea, just like your ma and me were friends and now we have four kids. Say something Sam."

"BJ, I seen that look in Josie's eyes. That same look was in Ann's eyes when I first walked into her café to try to sell her some beef. Yea, I'd say she's got it bad as I think you have."

"You two, don't you think we better get out on the range before the sun goes down."

"You know I think he's right boss, this time."

We mounted up and headed out to look over the ranch and as we rode that one thing kept coming back to my mind. Where was Martin? Then the horse I was riding jumped, I had put Blacky in the pasture with Lagger for a long rest. They were both old and had lived longer than a horse should and this new horse I didn't know as well as Blacky, anyway he jumped over a small creek that was dry this time of year with winter coming on. That jump brought my attention back to what Sam was saying.

"That creek we just jumped over dries up this time every year."

"It always has and the stock has to go an extra mile for water."

"You know Silver that's what I've been thinking so I've started the men diverting the water from that pond up yonder, cause it's most of the time still full and it's downhill from there to here. It would only take a small trench to let water flow this way and keep this creek with some water in it all year. If the pond started getting to low we could keep the gate at the pond closed that we would install."

BJ said, as he looked it over how the land sloped down to this point.

"Sounds reasonable to me. What you think pa?"

I was still thinking about what the sheriff might had found out about Martin.

"Pa, are you listening."

"Yea, Sam that would make sense and keep the weight on the cattle. Then we can keep a couple of mangers down here for the winter. Glad I thought of hiring you as foreman, old friend."

That brought a smile to Sam's face but I knew that Sam knew what I was really thinking about when he said.

"Silver, your mind's not here. Why don't you go to town and find out what John found out about Martin. Bills been waiting to talk to you about the mine for some time now."

"Pa, if Martin got lose we have all our men and the men from Josh's ranch and all the town's people. We can handle them."

"I just don't know. You saw BJ how he treated the people in Flagstaff. I don't want that happening to Durango if I can help it."

"Silver, I know you and you always take everything on your back and it always works out fine."

"This time may be the one time I can't handle it."

"It's on your mind so take off for town and put your mind at rest."

"You're right Sam, BJ you want to come along."

"Not this time, I think I'll hang around and listen to more of Sam ideas. If you don't mind."

"No son, one day grandpa and me will be gone and even old Sam here. That's when you and Bobby will have to take over. You'll have to know most about all this land to teach Bobby when he's old enough." As I said this my hand went up and waved around toward the land all around us.

I turned this horse that I wasn't used to and headed to town with one thing on my mind. As I rode away I heard Sam tell BJ.

"I hope everything is alright cause y'all have been through enough out there working undercover for the government."

I stopped and saw Blacky come up to the fence and I rode over. I always thought that Blacky knew what I was thinking and we had been through a lot together so it was my pleasure to unsaddle this dang blame horse and turn him loose in the pasture and bring out Blacky. Blacky reached down and took the saddle blanket up in his teeth and tossed his head back and I put the blanket on him along with my saddle that Foster had made me many years ago. That's when Foster walked up.

"Where you'se going old man?" As I turned and saw Foster and already knew who it was and knew I would never forget this old man's voice and his slang even when he was gone.

"Look who's talking about being old and for your information I'm going to talk to John and Bill." "You'se worried about Martin. I'se just knew it this morning after hearing Tomas yesterday and while you'se at saddling put a saddle on Lagger for me'se. I'se need to check on the shop and see how Gerard did with the work that I'se left him to do while we'se were away."

As we turned to head for town we saw Red Bird walking up.

"You going to town hon. I just knew you were worried."

"Does everyone around this ranch know what I'm thinking all the time?"

"I don't know about the others but I know when my husband is worried. You get along I will hook-up the buckboard and catch up."

"You want me to do that for you sweetheart."

"And who do you think did it when you were gone all those months?"

"Foster, it don't pay to come home when my wife has become too much like the white women around here even talks like them now."

Foster said as we rode off. "That's Jenny's doing, I'se told you'se so."

"I heard that Foster. I'll see you two in town."

This was the first time in these many months that I had ridden up Main Street of Durango. It was mostly the same but there were two new streets branching off Main with mostly new houses and some new shops. This must be the work of Tim and there he was walking down the street checking up on his men that were hard at work on what looked like a very large house. So I stopped to say hello to my partner from the mine. Foster said. "See you'se later, I'se don't want to hear him. He always thinks he'se so funny just like his partner." Foster went on down the street to his shop.

"Good to see you Silver." Tim said at almost the same time, as I was about to say the same as we shook hands.

"Looks like from the size of that new house y'all are doing well. Who you building it for?"

"Don't rightly know. Got a letter in the mail a month ago with $50,000 in it with no name on the letter. Just said he would need it for his niece and him when he got to town to start a business."

"His niece. Good to see you Tim. Tell Jim I'll be up to the mine now that things have calmed down; we'll have you over for supper some night. I need to talk to John."

I waved as I rode away over to John's office. As I started to go in Red Bird rode by on the way to who knows where and waved and smiled. I knew that smile it always comes to her face the morning after I'm back home from a long trip. As I turned away from Red Birds beautiful smile and started to turn the knob of the door to John's office all hell broke loose all at once. Ten men came riding down the street shooting in every direction. I jumped down as I pulled my .45 to shoot back as John came out the door and took a hit in the leg as he was laying there he pulled his gun out shooting as fast as I was. Three of the men were out of their saddle and dying in the dust of the street. I saw two of the remaining men ride up to Red Bird and pull her out of the buckboard and go on down the street out of town. Two more were down and I jumped on Blacky and started after them as John shouted.

"Martin got away from the fort and most of his men with him."

I yelled. "Someone get the doc for John."

"Don't worry about me get after them they have Red Bird. This is just a scratch I'll be in the saddle later today. Now get."

As I headed to chase the kidnappers Foster came running out of his shop along with Gerard, the new man in town and I yelled at him.

"They got Red Bird. Get the men at the ranch and follow my trail. Tell BJ, Martin got away from the army. He'll tell Josie and Tomas will see that she's all right. Send someone to Josh and tell him to get his men on my trail."

I didn't know how many men Martin had now but they had my wife and nothing would stop me from getting her back. Martin just made the biggest mistake of his life and his life would be mine. The trail took a turn toward the northwest and that was towards the mine. The trail wasn't hard to follow with five horses and I could tell which horse was carrying Red Bird cause the same track was all over the trail sometimes going way in front and other times lagging behind. I knew they had a big problem on their hands. They seemed to only be two mile or so ahead as Blacky took to the chase as I knew their trail and their horses after studying their hoof prints. So I let Blacky have his head and he was off to the races. He had slowed down as he aged but he could still out last any horse on the range. Foster's old cabin wasn't far ahead and as I had thought as I circled around the cabin there was a horse in the back of the cabin with its reins hanging in the dirt. I knew that they might have left someone here to ambush me but as I got closer there was a moaning sound coming out of the cabin on the quiet breeze from the north. I pulled my .45 and creep to the back of the cabin. Blacky was left by this fellow's horse, which kept him quiet. There was no sound except that moaning so I crawled on hands and knees with my .45 in one hand to the front of the cabin under the window that was half broken out. Peeking inside over the ledge there by the bed on the floor laid a young man with his hands over this stomach still moaning with his eyes closed. A gun was nowhere in sight so shoving my gun in the holster at my right side I threw open the door and the young man's eyes popped open in surprise as I rushed to his side. I said as I bent to check his wound. He didn't look much older than BJ.

"Who are you? And where are the others going?"

The wound was bad and if he were still alive in a couple of hours he would be lucky. He didn't say a word till I told him.

"Son, you're gut shot and won't live to see sundown again. You picked the wrong man to follow. I'm sorry."

"Please do something for me, I lost my gun a ways back. It hurts so bad and I knew when I felt the pain I was a goner. Heard what gut shot means to a man."

I knew what he meant by that so I put the pillow that was left on the bed under his head.

"I can't do much for you and they have my wife."

"That was your wife we took."

"Yes son, where are they headin'?"

"You must know by now cause you must be Silver Buck if that's your wife. Since I'm dying I'll tell you. Martin and the men took over____

That was all that the boy said as his head hung down to his side and he wouldn't have any more pain. As I reached Blacky there were horses coming up my back trail.

I mounted and held Blacky in as he was ready to be let loose as Foster and our men came riding up with their horses just starting to lather up.

"Foster, your horses need rest. Bury the boy in your cabin. He tried to tell me something but he didn't get to finish but it's for sure they're heading for the mine with Red Bird. I'll be on my way."

"Josh's men are behind us and BJ flew south to get Peso and I'se sent a man to Dancing Bear village. You'se don't go rushing in there before we'se get there. You'se gets you killed. That's what Martin wants. So just stay away till everyone gets here and we'se think of a plan."

"Foster, he's got my Red Bird."

"I'se know son but---

I didn't hear the rest of what Foster said as Blacky raced away toward the mine. The tracks were plain in the dirt, they wanted me to know which way they were heading as I flew through the forest on Blacky's back I thought about what Foster had last said. "That's what Martin wants." This repeated in my head over and over as Blacky ran closer and closer toward the mine. Now I got some of my calm back. I patted Blacky on his neck and slowed him to a trot as we came closer.

"Blacky boy I'm starting to understand what Foster was trying to get me to understand."

We were now two or two and a half miles from the mine and by now they were there with Red Bird. I left Blacky to his self and left the reins tied around the pommel so they wouldn't get caught up somewhere. Grabbed my 44-40 out of the scabbard and I took off on foot through the forest up the side of the mountain but I moved toward the backside of the mountain for I knew every inch of this place. I was looking for lookouts that I knew Martin would have posted mostly on three sides around this mountain. As I cleared through some of the undergrowth I could see two men sitting on top of two different boulders two hundred feet apart. They could easily be picked off with my rifle but I didn't want to warn Martin I was near so I went on and would remember where all the lookouts were. I went around the backside where no men had been posted then to the other where I found two more guards. Starting back to where I had left Blacky for I had seen enough to make a plan for an assault on my own mine. As I passed toward the front of the mine low down in some of the brush that had grown up where we had cut down the trees to build the cabins many years ago, there was Martin out in front of the office pacing up and down with Jim there with a guard that had a gun in his back and Red Bird was there near out of sight on the other side of the office with her hands tied but looked alright. I could have killed him right then and there but didn't know what the guards would do to Red Bird or Jim and I couldn't take that chance. As I crawled on down the side of the mountain I knew that Foster had to be near now and probably had found Blacky and waited for me.

As I came near there were the men and Foster talking to Tim walking up and down with his hands behind his back. Then I came out in the open to some of Foster's fury. He looked at me and they all came toward me.

"I'se thought you'se was going to be a fool and rush them by you'se self. We'se was about to rush in there right after you'se. You'se never a hot head till it comes to Red Bird."

"I know and I did hear you and started to think. I scouted around the mine and they have guards posted on three sides but not the backside. I saw Red Bird and Jim they look like they hadn't been hurt but the men were nowhere in sight. We have to find out where the men are and where they keep Red Bird and Jim tonight before we do anything. How's John? I hated to leave him like that, but they had Red Bird."

From out of nowhere came a voice.

"John's alright, the doc told me to stay in bed but I never do what he says anyway and he knows that. Told you I'd be in the saddle later today." John was walking up to us slowly with a limp and a cane in his hand.

"Nobody tries to take over our town and gets away with it. Did you see the rest of his men?"

"No, just about ten or so. The rest must be guarding my men."

"I don't think so. Before I left Tomas, you know that old Comanchero you brought among us."

"When did you find that out? I'm so worried I forgot I told you at the ranch."

"After that raid. Tomas came to me with BJ and Josie and told me more about his self. Anyway he said that's the way Martin starts with a small raid to draw the people with a knowledge of weapons away from town while most of his men will take over the town and intimidate the people that don't carry guns till they give up while the others are away chasing the first raiders."

"So what are we going to do? I have to get Red Bird and all the men out of there safe."

13

"Silver, you don't worry. We'll get the men and Red Bird out safe. I made Tomas and BJ deputies and put them in charge of defending the town. Josie was getting all the women together to show them what to do to help. She had seen the shortcomings of some of her uncle's plans in Flagstaff after you left. She said the women rose up with the men and they helped run Martin and his men out of town thanks to the rifles you left behind."

"You think BJ and Tomas can handle the situation?"

"They can with the General's help. General Cook came riding into town about an hour after BJ got back from telling Peso. That big Mescalero beats all he was riding right alongside General Cook proud as can be. Cook interpreted what he said.

He told everyone around that Buck Taylor saved his live so he came to save big town from Comancheros. He brought along fifteen warriors."

"That's Peso, he just wants to be at peace but knows that sometimes you have to fight for that peace."

Bill Gills had come riding up from town. He was the last that came with John.

"What you doing here?"

"The towns in good hands and I didn't get to talk to you in town with what went on. We need to talk about the mine."

"Bill, not now we have to get the men and Red Bird out of there."

"I know but doc said after John left that before one of the Martin men died he told doc that Martin planned to blow up the mine. Martin said you blow up his riches so he was going to blow up yours with your wife and friends."

"We have to get them out right away. I don't care about the mine it's our people we have to save."

"That's what is important I got this report from a mining engineer that I hired cause the mine was producing less and less every month. Here's the report."

I took it from Bill's hand and started to read.

To Mr. Gills:

> The mine has been depleted of most of the silver. There are little pockets left but I do not think that it is worth continuing operations for the small amount that would be gained. I am truly sorry for this news.
>
> Yours as always
> Benjamin Beckman

I felt stunned at the news. Gone after twenty years but that was not in my mind right this moment. Then a thought came to my head and I called Foster and Tim over. "Old partners this is the worst news but it brought back in my mind. You two remember back many years ago when the mine was producing less and you started tunneling from the back side and it met the main tunnel but it didn't pan out."

"Sure Silver I remember, that's when we discovered the large pocket to the north and abandon that tunnel cause it showed no sign of silver."

"Is that entrance still there?" Foster spoke up as he got through rubbing his head in the way he always did when he was thinking.

"I'se remember that we'se blocked that entrance with dead trees and brush so the varmints would stay out especially the skunks. That summer we a passel of them. But I'se know it's there somewhere."

"Tonight we're going to scout out where they are keeping our people."

As I was talking into our mist came up on us without a sound Dancing Bear and five of his braves.

"Daughter and men have in mine and other men in large teepees made of wood like town."

I went to Dancing Bear and took his hand in mine and shook it.

"Always like Buck Taylor, my son way to greet Dancing Bear."

"They have Red Bird."

"Braves scout out mine."

"Foster, the men in the cabins has to be Martins for he would want them better off than our men. Red Bird must be with them. We'll find that old tunnel tonight and get everyone out then let Martin blow the whole place up far as I care." Tim stopped me as I was talking about blowing up the mine.

"Silver, Martin has to have every part of the mine full of dynamite if he wants to blow it up. We'll have to be extra careful when we go in there."

"The day is near gone we better get planning." I said as we saw the shadows of the trees get longer through the forest as we stood there in the waning twilight before night dropped its black curtain over us as I thought that the mine might all be gone in an instant but it didn't matter as long as we saved everyone from the clutches of the Comancheros. The night would be pitch black for the moon was not going to be up till a couple of hours before dawn as the night before. No fires would be burning into the night. Martin had to know we were out here somewhere for his men left a clear path for us to follow, that had to be on purpose to draw me into his web of outlaws, but we weren't going to let him know where we were. I brought the men together even Dancing Bear and his braves were there. I now had a cool mind and was ready to attack Martin silently as before.

First Dancing Bear you know what your braves can do. We need all the guards around the mine out of the way permanently and silently as I know you can do."

"Uga, me know what Buck means."

"Foster and Tim you go with me to find that old opening to get in the mine. You two know that mine better than anyone alive." They looked at each other.

"That we'se do Silver even in the dark."

"The rest of you get as close as you can without being detected. Martin has more than fifty men and we don't know where they all are so if you hear a signal, which you'll know to start firing into the camp as we have gotten everyone out. If you don't hear a signal by near dawn come back here and we'll have to think of another plan."

Bill spoke to us. "Martin's men, at least most of them might be on their way to Durango."

"They will have a big surprise with the General and his men there along with Peso and Tomas that knows the ins and outs of Martin's mind and BJ with Josie that all so knows her uncle."

Tim led the way with Foster close behind and me last to watch our back trail. Tim gave the guards a wide berth and it was onto an hour before we make it to the spot where the entrance might be. Tim told us in a whisper.

"Now find and seek cause it's been many years since we dug this."

We parted ways but not too far apart to find that opening. The dark made it doubly hard and we had to be quiet. I pulled at brush and bushes for a hundred yards and then moved up and worked my way back and nothing. We were searching for almost two hours when we hear two guards coming. As they came closer we heard a small sound "whish" and then other. Then the guards were gone out of our sight till I stumbled over their bodies lying face down in the dirt. Then I heard a small sound and worked my way toward that sound, it was Foster and Tim pointing at some brush that I know I had passed before. We reached and started pulling the brush away from a large hole and there was the huge trees piled up to the top in the hole. It took all three of us to lift each log. Trying not to make a sound and as we removed more logs we heard a sound coming from within the mine. Then we saw a small light shining out toward the dark. Just as I was climbing into the mine a hand reached out for mine and then there was Jim's big smile starring me right in the face as the light was shining on him.

"Looks like we both had the same thought."

"Did any men get hurt when Martin's men attacked you?"

"No, we weren't expecting any attack so all our guns were in the cabins so we had to give up any fight. But Silver, Martin has this mine rigged full of our dynamite. Every tunnel is loaded and it all leads to one place that he said he would light if we tried anything foolish."

"Where's Red Bird?"

"I haven't seen her; the boys and I didn't even know she was here."

"They kidnapped her from town."

"She has to be in the office cabin. That's where Martin should be. It's the only real nice cabin."

"Foster, you lead the men down the mountain and tell the others not to open fire just yet."

Tim and me watched as the men passed us going down to safety. As Paul passed us I heard him tell Tim.

"I hope you have plenty of guns and rifles down there that son-of-a-bitch threaten to blow up our mine and jobs with it."

"Where you get the candles?"

"Habit, always put four or five in my pocket every morning never know when you may need light in here."

"Can I have a few? We're going through the mine it's the quickest way to the office."

"Be careful he has guards everywhere and dynamite."

Tim and me worked our way through the tunnels of the mine with one small candle lit. Tim pointed out the dynamite as we came close to the entrance. I put out the candle and put it in my pocket. The guards were there but not to alert at this time of night and I could see the office, which still had a light shining out the window as I took a look out. The guards were smoking cigarettes as they talked to each other. They kept looking toward where we were standing but couldn't see inside the dark mine. We had to make a move before the sun started to rise. The half-moon was already up overhead, as I had to think of a way to get over to that office. I moved forward a few steps and the stones made noise so the guards came toward us as I picked up several stones and one by one threw them over the guard's head and after each stone hit the ground the guards would turn and walk the way of the noise. We pulled our guns and I motioned to Tim with the barrel in my hand to hit the guards. As I threw the last stone they turned quick and we went into action and the two men laid flat on the ground. The rope we used to tie them up with was their own from their horses standing right in front of the mine. We had to work fast as the light of dawn was coming up in the east as we made it to the corner of the office. Looking in the window there was Red Bird tied to the four corners of the bed while Martin was sitting in the chair by the desk looking at her with beady eyes. He was saying.

"It's hard to believe a woman as beautiful as you would be married to a man like Silver."

"He's more of a man than you ever thought of being."

"You speak English so well for a redskin. Now I'm going to show you what a real man can do for you."

I couldn't take it anymore as Martin moved toward the bed and my Red Bird.

"You stay here and give me twenty seconds to get to the front door and you break out the window then duck for your life."

I rounded the corner and I knew the front door was right there at the top of the stairs where I was, then I heard Tim break the window and at the same time I broke down the door and there was Martin taking aim at the window across Red Bird. I took a flying leap off the top of the inside stairs toward Martin just as his gun went off into the floor as I hit his gun hand and we went rolling on the floor as I was holding his gun hand. I saw Tim rush in the front door down the stairs.

"Get Red Bird and get out of here."

We were back on our feet when the war began with Martins shot in the floor our men started firing and I knew they were moving forward toward the mining camp to try to take it back. As Martin hit me a glancing right to the jaw I went rolling toward Tim and Red Bird as they were moving toward the door up the stairs. I yelled.

"Get her out of here to a safe place in the forest away from the shooting and the rigged mine."

I grabbed Martin's leg as he turned to beat Tim and Red Bird to the door but Tim knocked him back toward me as I was on my feet again.

As I hit Martin he went flying toward the door I glanced out the window and saw Red Bird was with Dancing Bear and Tim at the edge of the thick forest and they were moving away from the mining camp. Tim had stopped and reentered the fight with Martin men pouring out of ours men's cabins. Martin made it through the door, picking up matches lying on a table by the door as I regained my footing. As I reach the door I picked up matches and three more candles as Martin was already at the mine's entrance with a lit match in his hand so I rush to where Martin was and spun him around and caught him with a blew to the chin. Then I pulled him upright and hit him again and he flew back into the dark mine and he looked to be out cold. Tim came up with John limping as I heard the firing lessen down in the forest to the north. John said as he looked toward the sporadic firing.

"Our boys are trying to round up the ones that weren't killed or wounded in the first assault."

"Well John there's your man that started all this." I pointed to where Martin had been laying in the mine entrance but as we turned Martin was gone and the matches were gone that were beside his body. As I rushed inside the mine I yelled.

"Y'all get out of here and keep the men away Martin is trying to light the fuse to the dynamite the whole place might go up."

They turned and ran for the woods taking hold of men and they turned and went down the mountain as fast as they could. Then I saw Red Bird and Dancing Bear with his braves running behind Tim and now Jim was with them.

It was dark as night as I went into the mine after Martin. This time I wasn't going to let him get away. I reached in my pocket for a candle and could see that Martin was nowhere in sight as I worked my way deeper into the mine that I knew by heart which tunnel led where. As I turned the second corner there was Martin with a grin on his face and a burning match in his hand.

"I'm going to blow this whole place up and you'll have nothing left of Jeb's."

I drew my gun and fired twice and the burning match flew through the air as Martin grabbed his hand in pain. The match landed on top of the fuse that led to the dynamite. The fuse sparked up and started its trek to the different parts of the mine where all the dynamite was set up throughout the mine. Martin jump for it but I shot him in the leg and ran toward him to pull him out of the mine that was going to blow up any minute. I reached down for him and pulled him up but he swung at me hitting me on the chin and I was on my back looking at him running toward the entrance and I was up heading the same way but as I turned the corner I saw Martin take a wrong turn that went deeper into the dark mine. I didn't have time to go look for him so I yelled.

"Martin you're going deeper into the mine, come back this way."

I only waited ten seconds and left to the outside of the mine and was pass the cabins when the explosion happen and catapulted me through the air for fifty feet, dirt and rocks with pieces of trees were flying all around me through the air when I hit a tree about ten feet off the ground and slid down the tree to the ground. The blast had knocked me out for when I opened my eyes there was Red Bird and I was covered with dirt and the rest of the men were standing over me. Dancing Bear was the first to see my eyes open.

"My son strong and wake now."

Red Bird had her arms around my neck crying tears of joy as I came more aware and was looking around. Foster walked up and looked at me.

"I'se sure thought you were a goner this time when I'se saw you flying into that tree."

I was groggy but becoming more alert now that I got my thoughts together. The dawn had broken and the sun was shining bright down on us as I stood up and dusted off my clothes from being almost buried in the dirt from the mountain.

"How's everyone." Jim spoke as I looked around to see that the cabins were totally gone from the blast.

"Our men are fine some small wounds but no one was badly hurt but we can't find Martin and twenty-five of his men are dead the rest escaped mostly on foot. No time to saddle a horse with us a coming up the mountain at them. Most must had still been asleep when the dynamite blew. Are you alright I told you most of this before."

"Yea, my head's just a little fuzzy. I'll be fine in a few minutes." Red Bird still had her arms around my neck and said.

"Now I understand why Josie left that man. He's a monster."

"Look all over, we have to find Martin's body to make sure he didn't escape."

"He couldn't have you was at the only exit." John said as I started walking toward the piles of wood that were the men's homes.

"He went toward the other tunnel."

The men were all around us now and saw what the blast had done as I looked at them and knew I had to tell them what was in the letter from the mining expert.

"Men your cabins are destroyed and I have here in my pocket a letter from a mining expert that says the mine is close to being mined out. So I guess this is a good time to close the mine for good. Y'all will receive a big bonus but I'm sorry to say your jobs are gone."

We heard yelling and a big commotion toward the mountain where the dynamite blast had blown out one side of the mountain to who knows where. There was Foster and Jim running toward us with their hats in their hands and big smiles on their faces and now I could tell the hats were full of rocks. Then Foster was jumping up and down in front of me yelling something. Then he slowed down his speech as he caught his breath with Jim right beside him breathing just as hard from the run down the mountain.

"I'se tell you'se right now look at this. Mining expert, beans I'se say see what that there blast uncovered."

Then Jim broke in. "Foster knows and to me this looks much more rich than ever came out of this here old mine."

"What are you two going on about?"

"That blast has blown a hole straight down thirty feet or more where we had never dug before. Look, this is silver ore in our hats. This came from the edge of that hole."

Then Foster broke in again as Jim sat down in the dirt that stood four inches deep all around us.

"Don't you'se understand Silver the biggest pocket of silver was right under our feet. All these years we'se been walkin' on the mother lode."

"Men, forget what I just said we might even have to hire more men. Now we have to build your cabins back before winter sets in." I stood right in front of them and tore up the letter and threw it up in the air to be taken away on the mountain breeze.

The yells went up from everywhere with men grabbing each other with big bear hugs and jumping up and down. But we still didn't know where Martin was.

"Jim, we're heading to town I'll send up tents and food with more men to get this place back in shape." I took Dancing Bear by both arms as Red Bird stood by.

"Thanks for the help old friend. One day I'll do the same for you."

"We now go to village. Daughter comes, see mother soon misses you much after all these moons."

We reached town the next day and nothing had happen so as I told General Cook what had happen Bill was there listening and I saw from the look on his face that he couldn't believe what had gone on up on that mountain. The General shook my hand.

"I guess we'll be heading for the fort now that Victorio has been dealt with and will never trouble anyone again."

Peso came up with BJ as the General led his troops out of town. Peso signed.

"Peso, braves go to village much do but good at peace."

BJ and me were standing side-by-side son and father as we watched Peso and his brave's leave to the south as Red Bird walked up with Josie.

"I told her about her uncle and what went on up at the mine."

"Silver, I know my uncle and if they don't find his body he could be out there organizing his Comancheros for another attack on you as long as he is still breathing a breath of air."

"I know we can handle anything he does cause look at the mine now thanks to him."

The north winds started to blow in the cold air and times became settled once again in Durango as the mild fall turned into a bad winter as Christmas approached. The cattle so far were coating with the cold as the snow flew. They had their hay out on the range with the ponds frozen over which had to be broken up every day, so the cattle could have water, by the cowboy that stayed in the line shacks during the winter. During breaks in the weather food supplies would be taken out to them. This in its self-took on a life in its self when the snow was two feet deep or more. The cabins had been finished before the bad weather set in but the work in the mine stopped as the snow fell into deep drifts but they worked as much as the weather would permit. Josie lived in our house and BJ worked on the ranch with the other men and stayed in the bunkhouse at night as the two of them had become closer into the winter months. The expected happen after Christmas one snowy night with the fire blazing, this Christmas had been a huge affair as big or bigger that the Christmas after the cattle drive, BJ and Josie came with love in both their eyes. BJ started and couldn't get it out so Josie took over. We were prepared cause it was obvious how they felt about each other since her leaving her uncle Martin. We never found his body but no one thought he could had survived that blast that opened up the new vein that was larger than the original one that great grandfather Jeb had found. So Josie started and it seemed she knew exactly what to say.

"BJ thinks because my family has given your family so much trouble and I am two years older than him you might not approve of us two getting ----." Then she couldn't go on. Then the courage came back to BJ. He knew he had to be the man that as his father I knew he was.

"Mother, father we love each other very much and want to have your blessing for us to be married in the spring. There I said it." BJ sat down and Josie sat right next to him and they both were looking down at the floor looking worried at what we would say as sweat broke out on BJ forehead and Josie was ringing her hands.

Red Bird and me were smiling at each other trying to be serious as they were but inside we were trying not to laugh for we knew how they felt from the beginning. I spoke up, as the two of them looked so scared at what we would do, as Red Bird went to Josie and took Josie's hands in hers as I spoke.

"You two don't look so scared we knew this was coming. I could see how you two felt about each other even out on the trail when you saw her red hair and she was yelling at me across the river."

"But pa I didn't even know then. How did you?"

"Cause son that's how I looked at your mother when I first saw her standing there by the pond." Red Bird broke in with a little giggle.

"Josie, he was taking a bath and had to come out or freeze to death so I just stood there until he had to come out."

"Red Bird let's not tell them everything."

"Anyway from that minute I knew he was for me." Red Bird hugged Josie.

"Welcome to the family. Dear isn't that what you were going to say."

"Yes honey."

"Josie now we have something to plan during this long cold winter. We may even get to go to town to let everyone know."

"Y'all two have your fun we men will sit back and relax by the nice warm fireplace." I told the women as they already had their heads together with an excited smile on both their faces. "No you will not, there will be plenty for you two to do during these cold months." Red Bird informed us out right.

"See, son how it is. You might as well get used to it. I don't know what happened to my sweet Indian Princess."

14

As the winter went by and the days became longer and the cold started to draw it's icy fingers back up into the high mountains the list for us men to do grow by leaps and bounds. We did everything the women wanted for we loved them.

I took a long chance without telling anyone. With the mine in full operation as it began warming Tim and me got together and planned a house to be built on the other side of Foster's house toward the mountains side. It would be a good ways away from all of the other houses on the ranch but a short ride by horse which we found out Josie loved to ride so for Christmas BJ had given her a sweet little filly from Jake's fine herd of horses and had broken the mare himself behind everyone's back. Josie had named it Snowflake for the filly was white as the soft power that falls during a mild winter day. Tim tried to talk me out of it.

"You know women, they like things the way they want them to be."

"I know but remember when Red Bird first saw the house."

"Yap, I do and she was scared at first. She never had seen such a thing. You remember Carolyn and Jenny they picked out all the house furnishings and changed the plans a dozen times before we were finished."

"You're saying not to do it?"

"No, just ask Josie how she feels about living so close to everyone and if she would like a house. Get her input."

"Then it's not a surprise."

"It's better to have your new daughter happy than surprised."

"You could be right as rain."

When I brought up the subject Josie was very surprised and Red Bird was glad I had asked Josie to get with Tim too find a spot for the house that she loved and tell Tim the way she wanted it built. At least I came up with the idea and so the house went up as planned without my input.

Josie and Red Bird were having the time of their lives picking out things for the house but BJ and me had little to do with it. We weren't even asked.

The week of the wedding came in April and the town was all a buzz. The town of Durango was now calling me a founding father that new label was added to Silver Buck as the headline of the new Durango Star read.

Son of Founding Father Silver Buck Taylor to be Married.

I found it to be outlandish but most liked what they read as I walked into Bill's office that was near as big as the bank.

"Bill, I don't like that title the newspaper stuck on me now. The Silver Buck that Foster stuck on me was way back and I thought it would go away but it hasn't. I didn't help start this town. That was done by better people than me."

"Buck, what are you talking about. This is modern times and if you hadn't come here twenty-two years ago this town would be just a little town in the foothills of the mountains and I would still be working at the bank and probably wouldn't be married to my lovely wife and have three beautiful daughters."

"You should be thankful they look like Jenny and not you."

Now Silver. Just look at old Foster is an upstanding part of this town. Let me tell you that would never have happen without you coming here. What you have done for the town is to many to list. You're just to humble Buck Taylor. Your sons and daughters are going to be a big part of this town's future. We are coming toward a new century."

"Alright, but if I'm always introduced as Founding Father Silver Buck something's going to blow-up in me one day."

"Buck, you're just too nice for that to ever happen."

"Well, I'm still the fastest man on the draw in this state. I still practice every day."

"The time of the outlaw is near over."

"I hope so but you never know do you."

"We'll see."

Tomas at this time had always been beside Josie watching her at every turn as her wedding day came near. This also was when Josie and Red

Bird were riding to town every day for wedding dress fixings of which there were many. Ann wanted to get the dress just right. Tomas had let me know what his feelings were when Martin's body was never found.

"Senor Buck, you not know Senor Martin, I think he could walk through Hell and come out alive. He is meaner than the Devil himself. The Devil could have taken lessons from him to be sure."

"Now Tomas, has anything happen these last six months since the mine blast except more men are now working in the mine all year round again and the town is attracting more business."

The day I came out of Bill's office talking to him about the article in the paper there was Josie and Red Bird, this time riding in the wagon must be takin' home more things for the wedding, going into Ann's store for the umpteen time but then I noticed Tomas was nowhere in sight. There was a tap on my left shoulder and I almost jumped out of my skin.

"Tomas don't do that." He just stood there with that big grin on his face.

"Could have been Martin."

"Would you forget about Martin? He's dead and buried under a ton of rock up at the mine. You'll see one day they'll fine his bones down deep under the mountain that came down on him."

"Senor Buck, I sure do wish I could forget but I can't when I see three of my old compadres horses tied at the rail in front of the saloon and I see them walk in the swinging doors in broad daylight like they have nothing to hide just three days before your son's marriage to Martin's Niece. But this was not his way of taking over a town that he wanted and Tomas thinks this town is one he really wants bad."

I was wearing my gun on my hip as I always have since the "old days" as Bill puts it. The anger could be felt moving up to my head but I had to calm down.

"Would you stand at my side when I talk to them. They will see you and know their plans can't work like Martin's."

"Tomas will go but we need to find Martin."

I saw John and we three walked to the saloon together. As we threw open the doors the smell was the same as I remember and the room was filled with smoke. The three men turned at the sound of us entering even above the noise that filled the place. We were within five feet of them. They had their backs turned to the bar and had whiskey glasses in their hands. Those smiles were wide across their faces as they saw Tomas.

"Tomas, Martin wondered where you went after Josie was stolen out from under his nose. I told him you went with her but he would not believe she and you would leave him."

"So Martin is alive." I said as their whiskey glasses hit the bar and were left alone.

"Not now, he was killed in that mine explosion can't you remember that far back Silver if I can call you by that outlandish name. You stole that mine from Josie's father and we all know the real truth." Then John spoke with the five-pointed star pinned to his shirt.

"You three need to get out of town. I have no proof that you were at the mine holding Silver's wife hostage or you three would be in jail."

"I know you are here for Senor Martin, scouting out the town."

"Tomas, Tomas you are filled with delusions. Everyone knows our beloved leader left this world in that blast. Now we three left Martin three days before to watch over Mr. Martin's interests in other places." This was said with a sad face and their hats in their hands covering their guns. I motioned for John and Tomas to move back with my hands to their chest. As my hands came away the three dropped their hats to the dirty floor and reached for their guns. Mine was out a split second sooner as fire erupted from my gun three times as they hit the floor. The smoke from my gun filled the room as the place was so quiet that I could hear the leader was still breathing. John knelt down to him as he was trying to speak.

"I always heard you were fast but never dreamed it was true." Then Tomas said as he bent down.

"Juan, is Martin still alive and somewhere around here?"

A smile once again came across his face and the smile disappeared once again as his head fell to the side and his eyes closed forever.

That afternoon I brought men in from the range to scout all around the town for miles. Even the next day the search went on and the time was running out fast. The wedding was to be at the church the next day at noon with the reception at the ranch afterwards. That night before the day of the wedding men were posted on most high points around Durango as a precaution. The night had been warm and calm but just as the light of dawn appeared in the east a strong blast from the north came rushing down the mountainside and a huge cloud of dust was coming in from the west at the same moment. Pete was sent to wake me but I was already out of bed and had Blacky saddled when Pete came into the house yard. I took one look at Pete's face.

"Get all the men in their saddles and ready to go and send Joe to Jake's and the other ranch's. Tell them this is to keep Durango alive."

Pete left for the bunkhouse and I heard Pete say something to someone and I turned to see who could be there. BJ was walking up strapping on his gun and with his bullwhip wrapped around his shoulder as always.

"Pete said they were coming from the west. I'll saddle Red and we'll be off."

"Son, this is my fight to end all that is bad between the Walters and the Taylor's. I love you riding beside me but this is going to be you and Josie special day. She doesn't need you getting hurt or killed."

"Pa, I know all that but that is why I need to do this. I need to show Josie that I can protect her from anything and one day a long ways away my brother and sisters will be running this ranch and the town needs to know a Taylor will always be here for them like you always have. Josie would expect no less of me."

"You are growing into some man that I will always be proud of. Get Red and we'll be gone."

I stood at this spot and looked out over the ranch that started as a vision in my mind. This had been once owned by Dan Walters Josie's father, just a corner of it out by the entrance. Now it spread down to the New Mexico border where Peso and his people were now starting a new life of peace. BJ and the men pulled me out of my thoughts as I took Blacky's reins up and pulled myself into the saddle.

"Blacky old boy, here we go just one more time."

BJ, Tomas and me led the men out of the ranch gate with my father and Sam beside us and as we rode men from all the different ranches would join us as we rode into Durango. The word had spread as we saw towns men and women coming out with their rifles and shotguns heading to the west end of town. John joined us with his healed leg. At the west end of town as we came near a barrier was starting to go up and I said to John over the sound of the horse's hoofs and the people yelling out orders.

"You staying here or coming with us?"

"I missed the first fight with this Martin and by God I won't miss this one. Gerard and Bill can handle it. I made them both deputies for this little fracas. Foster ready did get a good man there and as for Bill there's none better. Where is Foster? I've never known him to miss a fight. "

"I didn't bother him he's near ninety now and that desert was so hard on him."

As we left town the barrier closed in the middle behind us and there I saw Foster riding like the wind as he flew over the barrier on Lagger's back. Foster rode up and John was laughing.

"I guess you can't pull one over on this old man."

"You'se bet you'se bottom dollar you'se can't. What you'se mean Silver leavin' me'se like that? We'se has been in ever fight together since we'se met. Juanita saw what was going on and shook me awake."

"You're here now and look who's coming in now."

Josh was riding up from the north and as I looked the dust that we were raising into the bright morning was enlarging as we keep riding Josh asked.

"How far off are they now?"

"We'll find out soon. Here comes Jock that first spotted them."

We could see Jock riding fast down from the pinnacle in the foothills of the mountains. As Jock rode up we were how a group of about seventy-five strong all use to hard work and all good or better with firearms when need be.

161

"Silver, they're about three miles off and I saw the leader. Doesn't look like any man I've ever seen."

"What you mean, Jock?"

"He has no hair not even eyebrows. Not even wearing a hat to protect from the sun. Something happened to his ears and nose with near no lips to speak of." I said.

"John, that has to be Martin. Must had been caught in that mine blast after all. That's why it took him this long to try to take revenge on us."

"There's a clearing over the next rise that we can spread out to meet them to show them our force."

Now all the men that had been posted all night came in and our ranks grow to ninety strong as we rode over the rise and took our places across the once lonely dusty road. Now we waited for what was to come in four long rolls looking to the west at the dust cloud coming at us rapidly. Boulders were all around us as we waited and men were up on top of each one with rifles butts resting on their thighs ready to be put into action. We were seven or so miles from town. This would give the town enough warning if we were overwhelmed for the shooting could be heard from town. The only sound that could be heard down the line of men were their horse's that knew something was going to happen so were nervous as we waited. The whinny of the horses was sweet through the air of the early morning with the dew hanging heavy on the air like an orchestra practicing before a performance.

One man on top of a boulder waved with his rifle in his hand so now they were very near. We would not fire on them unless they fired first and the thought never would have occurred to any one of us. Another man up on top started raising ten fingers and continued to open and close his hands twelve times so we now knew we were outnumbered by at least thirty men. The air was now full of tension as Blacky and Red started stamping their hoofs in the road that made the dust rise into the calm, clear skies. The time was upon us as the first man was seen coming around the bend in the trail with boulders on each side sticking up toward the clear blue cloudless sky. The heat was tremendous for this time of morning and the dew had left with the rising sun.

The figure that rode forward toward us had no resemblance of a face of a man. He rode right up to us unafraid and in total defiance of the law. John spoke as Martin stopped in front of us with his men filtering out from around the boulders.

"You are Jeb Martin?"

"Yes, sheriff I am and very nice to meet you."

"You and all your men are under arrest for murder and mayhem across the southwest and Colorado. The United States government has a warrant for your arrest."

"I don't have any idea what this is all about. I was on my way to my niece's wedding in Durango." Here is where I spoke to Martin.

"You know Martin that Josie doesn't want you there. You are all done bullying people. She is a decent human being not like the rest of your family. I think the last decent Walters was your wife and she's dead."

"Regrettably my wife is gone now but she never understood what had to be done to get ahead in this world. I see you have to speak for the little pup of yours. He has to be a man if he's going to marry a Walters." Now BJ spoke to the deformed figure in front of us.

"You just get off that horse mister and we'll see who's the man."

"I don't resort to personnel violent and anyway a little accident has kept me under the weather for some time now and this is the first time I've been out since then."

As we spoke his men were trying to surround us as our men from up above kept an eye on the proceeding with rifles across their saddles ready for trouble. Our men spread out wider apart.

"This is getting us nowhere. You going to come with us to the fort for trial or end it right here." John told Martin as he directed the men to get ready for anything.

"Tope, it's nice to see you. I could have killed you back in Flagstaff but for some strange reason I liked you with your big smile. I thought you may had learned your lesson and left this madman as Tomas has."

"We were wondering where you disappeared Tomas. Good men are hard to find now days."

"Senor Martin Tomas is unafraid of you now. Leave Josie alone."

As Tomas ended I saw Tope move toward his gun and as Martin saw Tope's movement he said "No, Tope." But it was too late and my gun and BJ's gun was out as Tope's gun was starting to rise. BJ bullet took Tope out of his saddle and two slugs came out of my gun as fast and caught Martin in both arms as he was trying to reach for his gun but it was too late as Martin fell from his saddle and his foot caught in the stirrup and his horse started to run as Martin was yelling at the top of his lungs his men started shooting but with our five men up high they didn't have a chance. My range hands and Josh's men were the best at what they did and that was to protect our property and lives. When the shooting was stopped what was left of Martin's men raised their hands and gave up as they saw all the empty saddles around them. We had ten men wounded but only one serious. John took care of the burial of Martin's dead and Josh told his wrangler's to round up all the loose horses and take them to the ranch and get to town for a wedding. John and five of my men were all that were needed to take what was left of Martin's men to town for the jail. BJ and me rode up to John as they were ready to go to town.

"John, we have to fine Martin and if he's alive we'll bring him in and if not we'll bury him. We can't take a chance that he got away again."

"BJ don't forget your wedding at noon. I sent Pete ahead to town to tell everyone to get ready for a hum-ding of a wedding and party. I hope you don't mind."

"No John we don't mind and how could I forget, got my suit right here in my saddlebags. If I have to I'll bathe in the creek and dress out here. I wouldn't miss marryin' that wonderful, beautiful, red headed woman for my life."

We headed out following the drag marks that Martin's deform body made in the dry dirt. As we went the brush had been knocked down and we could tell after two miles that Martin had not shook loose of the horse. There were rocks in the trail that were covered with blood as we went on the brush was covered with his blood and as we spotted the horse we approached slowly as not to spook him again. I worked my way around giving the horse a wide berth. I left Blacky and walked up and grabbed the horse's reins as BJ came walking from behind. There was Martin still hanging from the stirrup and there was no movement as I unhooked his boot away from the horse's stirrup. As I settled down the horse I saw BJ looking down at the mangled body that once had been a human being. We started to dig the hole to put Martin's body in BJ finally spoke to me.

"How can people become so mean and want money so bad to come to this?"

"I don't know son if it's just evil reaching out to some or if their mind is somehow so distorted to make them think that they deserve anything everybody else has."

As we laid Martin to rest out in a valley that rested between two small hills we made a small marker with his name and that is all. As we rode off I turned in my saddle.

"BJ we better find that creek, that redheaded woman's not going to wait for you all day."

"I think you're right pa."

We slapped Blacky and Red on their rumps and down the valley we went looking for a creek as we rode toward town.

As we enter Durango from the west in our fresh clothes and clean bodies even our hair was clean under our hats. The three-day growth of beard was gone from our faces. The town had changed since this morning for all the barriers were gone from Main Street and the people were hurrying toward the church with not a gun in sight as both of us had put our guns away in our saddlebags before coming into town. It was near noon as we rode up in front of the church and there I saw pa and ma coming toward us as I spotted Peso with Solie and Juan, then the biggest surprise was Dancing Bear and Red Birds mother were both standing by Peso with only Red Bird in between. Pa said in a hurry.

"BJ you're almost late. You and Buck go around back and enter through the backdoor." Then ma added:

"Hurry now Josie will be riding up in the buggy any minute and you can't see her until she comes in the church."

As we hurried I stopped and shook Peso hand and hugged and kissed Red Bird and her mother then gave Dancing Bear a big bear hug as he smiled and said.

"Meet Grandson woman real nice and me like all red hair."

"Thank you, grandfather but pa we have to hurry I see the buggy coming from the ranch and Foster is driving."

"Son, turn away you don't want to see Josie." Red Bird said as we turned the corner for the backdoor.

15

We entered and took our places by the preacher as I looked the church was full as the front of the church was except for the front roll where all our family would sit down before Josie entered. Neither one of us had been told who was giving Josie away. Then the church doors open and BJ and me looked on as our whole family was being escorted to the front roll even Peso and Solie with Juan were sitting by Dancing Bear. I was going to have to find out what happened this morning after we left to make those two former foes just by the tribe they belonged to, to become what looked to be friends as they sat there together. My thoughts came back to the front of the church as I saw BJ look for Josie coming in, he looked so nervous. But it was Summer coming down the aisle spreading flowers in front of her. I looked across where Josie would be standing was sixteen-year-old Song Bird and it took me back to when she was born and we had named her Lady Bird. One day after, when Dancing Bear came to see his new granddaughter he told us a story about a dream he had the night before. In the dream Dancing Bear was asleep under his favorite tree under the stars in the twilight of the night when a bird woke him singing a beautiful melody that he had never heard. He called it the Song Bird and it was an omen that his first granddaughter had to be named Song Bird so her name was changed when she was one day old to Song Bird and it was true she always has sung like a songbird.

Now came Robert or Bobby as he has come to be known at school with the pillow with the rings. He took his place behind his brother and me. This is when the wedding march began and into the church came Josie escorted by Foster of all people and he had a smile all across his face. I could tell he was so proud to have been asked to do this. I noticed BJ as I put my hand on his shoulder and he took a glance at me for a moment with a huge grin on his face and they turned to watch his bride come toward him on Foster's arm. The music stopped, as Foster and Josie stood right near us as the preacher began.

"Who gives this lovely woman away?"

"I'se do." Foster said with that big smile across his face and then stepped back and sat in between Red Bird and Peso. The wedding continued as all the wedding before ending with:

"You can now kiss your new bride."

The church inside and out went up with applause as BJ kissed Josie in front of us all. I stepped forward and yelled over the applause.

"Everyone is invited to the ranch for a hum-ding of a party that will be hard to outdo for many years to come."

BJ and Josie was the first to leave for the ranch in the buggy I had bought when our three friends got married to their lovely brides many years ago. I went to Red Bird and told her while our whole family was standing by.

"Honey, this is what we started many years ago when you caught me bathing in the pond. Who knew that this would happen from that moment in time."

Most laughed cause over the years Red Bird had repeated that story many times. Even Dancing Bear was grinning as I signed to Peso the story about the pond and bath and a grin came over his face. Then I signed again.

"Now Peso and you Solie know that story you two and Juan are now part of our family." Peso gave me a great big hug. Everyone headed for the ranch for our son's wedding party.

I rode beside Dancing Bear and Peso on the way to the ranch and had tied Red behind the buggy. Red Bird and the children were in with Juanita next to Foster as he drove. When we reached the ranch the sight of wonder was before me in front of our home. There were about fifty lodges that had been erected since this morning. I rode up to Red Bird.

"You have to tell me how you got those two to stay this close together and they are acting like friends."

"Darling, I'll tell you later and they are not acting. They are friends forever."

I was amazed at the transformed ranch of this morning. All the women in town must had come and helped for the huge barn was decorated from the ground with red, white and blue bunting and a huge sign over the barn door that said:

"Congregations Newlyweds"
April 12, 1894
A Dated To Remember Forever
BJ and Josie Taylor

Red Bird and me entered the barn and there were people all around and cakes and pies were very much in attendance with the biggest punch bowl there had ever been. The barbeque was on the open pit to the side of the barn. Juanita, Juan and Manuel had out done their selves with Mexican style potato salad, beans and loads of rice. The music was starting and the newlyweds were on their way from the house with a line of people on both sides of the path from the house to the barn. They were being showered with more confetti that had ever been seen in the west. Josie and BJ had their hair and clothes covered and the biggest smiles in the world. They looked so happy and I realized that Josie now knew she was truly wanted and loved by her new family as they entered the barn. This was their time to enjoy their start of a new life together. I pulled Red Bird outside where it was quieter and looked at her in her beautiful black eyes after I kissed her.

"Now, you have to tell me how you got those two together."

"They showed up at the same time father from the north and Peso from the south. They had all their lodges with them as they stared at one another for the longest time and both even brought their braves up to a line in front of our house. I wasn't going to have a war in our front yard. Even Josie and the people from town looked worried about what might happen. We had just had word from Pete that the Comancheros had been defeated. I went out to father and to his lodge that mother and my sister had already put up and found his peace pipe. I stomped toward him and

I think he knew his daughter was full of fury. I stood in between them both and look at them and said.

"Dancing Bear my great father the man of peace that took his people away from others in the Ute tribe that wanted war with the whites but my brilliance father knew it was better to make peace with the white man. You met Foster and Jeb, Buck's great grandfather and they wanted to trade and the town of Durango started and you went to the people of the town and showed them you were peaceful. Then Buck, Foster and BJ found Peso staked out on an anthill by his own people the Mescalero's Apaches that had cut out his tongue for wanting the same thing that you wanted father many suns ago. Buck helped him and they have become good friends."

The two of them just stood there tall and proud as I talked about how good each of them were.

"Father this is a day that your first grandson is to be married. Peso, BJ and Josie you call friends."

I held out the peace pipe to father and he took it and sit with his legs crossed and motioned to Peso to sit and share the pipe. They saw that they were both Chiefs of their own tribes that both wanted peace with the white man and now with each other.

"You are my beautiful little diplomat. Let's go in and have my dance with our new daughter and you with your son and then we'll go down to the lodges and see how our new neighbors are doing."

"By the way Buck they're staying for a month."

"Well, why not we're just one big happy family with a lot of good friends."

We both had our dances and we kidnapped the newlyweds after explaining to all.

"They will be back but we have other family down yonder that we need to present the bride and groom to."

We two couples left the barn and headed to the lodges that had fires burning all around. We hadn't noticed until we were at the circle of lodges that near everyone had followed us down the way. We spread out to watch as the drums were beating and the braves were all painted in differ colors as they danced around the fires. Dancing Bear was informed that we were there and came out to greet us with Peso and Solie.

"Daughter you and whole family come sit and enjoy marriage dance. Now Grandson and bride here let ceremony began."

Dancing Bear took BJ and Josie by the hand and led them to the inner circle by the fire there he tied their legs together with a leather thong that held them tight as they hugged each other tight not knowing what to expect. Dancing Bear said in his language and then in English for the guess.

"With this bond now tied these two together which just like BJ mother and father and their mother and father this bond will never break and they will go through life happy with many children." Dancing Bear bent and untied the leather and handed it to Josie.

"This is for you always to keep to remember the promise you two made together on this day with full moon above and good friend all around you. Whites and Indians stand together this night proud and as one." Then Peso stepped forward and signed and BJ interpreted what he signed for everyone to know.

"Peso and wife Solie give to friends BJ and Josie these clothes that will remind them of our long and lasting friendship. They will last as long as deer's roam forest."

Josie had tears in her eyes as she held onto the beautiful Indian dress with moccasins and the leather that would keep them bound forever. Josie stood there silent for a moment then spoke to the crowd whites and Indians alike.

"My family has been so bad to this town, whites and Indians alike. Trying to take all that they could get from you. They are all died now and I have a new family. I came to this town and you treat me so good and this family that I have married into has taken me in as one of their own. For the rest of my young life I will do my best to show my thanks to everyone in this town that I understand the love that has been given freely to me."

Josie hugged and kissed BJ that had been next to her then she ran to Red Bird and Silver Buck and surrounded them with her arms with tears in her eyes. The party continued on into the night with Dancing Bear and

Peso entering the barn and watching how white people danced. Dancing Bear looked at his daughter and told her.

"Not so much different than Indian dance but our drums better." The people around them laughed and kept dancing into the night.

Later that night after BJ and Josie had been escorted to their new home to spend their wedding night and spend the rest of their lives together Silver Buck and Red Bird were standing on their front porch holding each other tight. The children, in their beds all worn out from the party as well as the Indians at rest in their lodges for the night as Buck spoke low so only she could hear.

"My dear love. Look out over all this. The lodges in our front yard and the mountains to the west and a town to the north that took us in as one of theirs. This was started years ago with the help of Foster and Jeb with your father Dancing Bear and the bond of friendship that they had. We need to do something special for those two one day. Foster, may not be with us much longer he's ninety or more now."

"We'll think on it tomorrow but right now let us enjoy being in each other's arms all night for you have been gone a long while."

On the way up the stairs to their room Buck asked.

"Where did Song Bird disappear to all night? I didn't see much of her."

Red Bird was holding Buck tight as they went up and told him.

"You haven't been around to notice our daughter is becoming a young lady. You know she's sixteen now."

"What does that have to do with the price of apples?"

"When Foster brought Solie and Juan to the house and you were gone with Peso. You know Song Bird became smitten with Juan and they spent lots of time together and have become close."

"You don't mean romantic."

"No, just good friends right now. She saw a tall good looking young man that is strong, not like the boys in school, and can take care of himself if he had to live off the land. She has never gotten to know the Indian way of living as BJ has learned from father. Right now it's just something new to her and they both just talk about their lives."

"I hope that's all because she's too young to think about leaving this house and she is older."

"Yes papa like Josie, now let's get in our bathtub and clean up and go to bed."

The month went by fast with Peso, Dancing Bear and me going hunting and talking. Taka was there also as Peso's second in command when I showed them the cattle of the ranch and how the men took care of the ranch. Then one day before they left Dancing Bear said.

"Me see ranch like village. Men are like braves, work all day and when trouble comes they stand with you as leader and fight to protect ranch and people."

"You know you're right. I never thought of it like that but you're right."

Then Peso signed, "Solie made pants and shirt for me to wear to wedding. Like it here but cannot get use to clothes. Skin has to breath. Cannot wait to get home."

I laughed and slapped Peso on the back. We rode on to the house as the sun was on its way down in the west behind the mountains and both of my friends were leaving in the morning. That night was another celebration but on a much smaller scale only the family and a few friends were there to say so long to our old family and new friends from the south. Red Bird and me were up and Foster was there as we stood and watched our family and friends take down their lodges and start to move out to their homes. BJ and Josie came riding up and they swung off their horses and went up to Dancing Bear and they both gave him a big hug and we saw tears come in his eyes as Peso walked up and BJ shook his hand and Josie hugged him and hugged Solie. BJ told them both.

"You two brave men are my family and if you ever need help of any kind send for me and pa and we'll come riding with any help you need."

Foster came up and put his arms around both and told them in his way.

"Dancing Bear, you'se and me been friends for now on to fifty years we'se were young men together. Now we'se are old but our friendship will last till the day we'se leave mother earth." He turned to Peso and put a hand on each of Peso shoulders.

"We'se are new friends but it will last till the last breath I'se take."

"Peso believes this also." Peso turned to Dancing Bear and signed.

"May come with son and wife one sun rise to village. Tell warriors my friends come for cannot forget traditions of the past. Warriors think enemy come but only friends of different tribe."

"Peso and family be welcome in my village, always."

I looked over to the side and saw Juan and Song Bird holding hands as we stood and waved as the two tribes parted and went to their villages to live in peace. Juan jumped on his bareback pony and caught up with his father at the head of their people.

That night BJ and Josie came upon the front porch where Red Bird and me were swinging in our favorite swing holding hands with my arm around my lovely wife. They sat across from us and BJ started.

"Now that everyone's gone we think that it's time we take you up on your offer for our honeymoon in Denver."

"That's a deal. When you want to leave. I have to go into town tomorrow I can get your tickets for the train." Josie spoke up, as we were swinging in the dusk of the evening.

"We thought day after tomorrow will do fine. Two weeks will be good to get away after all that my uncle put us through."

"I'll draw out some money for you to spend Josie. BJ won't be needing much."

"Now Buck, BJ might want something manly for their new home." Red Bird finally put into the conversation.

We four sat on the porch in the dark and enjoyed the night's coolness in the spring air. Song Bird came out and curled up against my side.

"Pa, what do you think of Juan."

"The cook in the bunkhouse?" She hit me on the arm lightly.

"Pa, now you know who I mean."

"He's going to be a fine man and brave to his people."

"He praises you and wants to learn the white man's way but he doesn't know what his mother and father will say."

"Song Bird, I don't know what to tell you. He can come here and learn some things but Peso I'm sure expects him to stay in the Indian traditions and way of life. That is between those two to work out and I'm sure they will find a way for Juan to do both if that's what he wants."

Song Bird kissed her mother and me and as she opened the door to the house she turned and said.

"I hope to marry him some day. He's so good and strong." Then she was gone as the door closed.

"What you think of that?"

"I told you Buck just puppy love. She will change over time."

"Pa sound to me she's got it bad."

"Look who's talking? Just got married and now he's the expert. Let's go to bed honey and leave these two-love birds to their selves. You know hun you were that age when we were married." Red Bird put her hand over her open mouth and then said.

"I forgot that!"

The next morning I rode Blacky to town for a meeting with Bill and Foster. Bill didn't say what he wanted but I guessed it was about the mine. As I walked in I saw that Foster was there with Tim and Jim.

"Shouldn't you two be at the mine or at least one of you?"

"I asked them to be here because they are partners and they have a report about the mine now here comes Sam the last partner. Now we're all here. Jim you are the day-to-day boss at the mine. You wanted to read what came from the mining expert this second time he's been out after the explosion."

"He says that he sees that the new vein goes straight down with branches coming off the main vein. He has no idea how far it may go. But for that kind of operation we need new and more modern machinery. I showed him the log for our shipments for the past twenty years and he thinks we can be shipping three times that much if we have the new machinery and if goes down as far as he think it does. We'll need twice as many men and more wagons and horses. This should cost $100,000 at the beginning to get going. The explosion took everything we had and turned it into debris."

"A $100,000, Bill that's a whole lot of money. This is the same man that told us to close the mine just three months ago and now it's just the opposite."

"Buck, as I told you we are now going into a new century. You always have taken risk and always won. What you say Foster?"

"I'se have my saddle shop and the money from the mine helps me'se keep it and I'se am an old man now so let you'se youngsters decide and I'se will go along for the ride."

"Sam."

"I say go for it what can we lose."

"Tim, Jim."

"We have our building business around town but more mining is still in our blood."

"I am the last and I want to do it for three times what we have taken out is around $20,000,000 for a $100,000 investment and put a lot more men to work. This town will really be put on the map. Buck, you and Foster started all this now don't you want to see it though. Your family will want for nothing for many generations and you may have them on the way before you know it."

"You're right Bill. If it falls through I still have the ranch. Foster lets go for it once more."

"Fine with me'se pard. I'se nearly feel like I did twenty years ago when we'se pulled out all that brush and there in front of us was what Jeb found."

We broke up the meeting and I went out with a smile on my face and a dance in my step as I walked into the railroad station and bought tickets for tomorrows train.

The next morning we loaded up the wagon and the whole family was off to town to see off the newlyweds on their honeymoon. Josie had just picked out a few new dresses she had received as wedding presents for she came to the ranch with not much to her name but Red Bird and Ann fixed that with an announcement in the newspaper. Ann's store was flooded with women buying the day before the wedding. We were looking at the results as the porters put Josie large trunk in the baggage car and the two were on the train and were off to Denver. As the train pulled out with our oldest child I held Red Bird tight as tears of joy ran down her face.

******

16

We worked our way down the crowded aisle of the passenger car to our assigned seats. As we moved along with Josie in front of me we passed several people that I knew since I was a child. As we passed a man tapped me on the shoulder and as I turned there was Mr. Winslow.

"Hello Mr. Winslow. Dear this is Mr. Winslow pa's longtime friend and banker."

"Hello my dear. Off to have a great time in the big city."

"I hope so sir. I haven't seen a big city since I lived in Boston when I was growing up."

"I go every month on banking business for a couple of days."

"You should bring your wife some time and spend a week."

He laughed as we took our seat.

"I don't think she could stand the heat in this blasted car this time of year. Maybe when fall gets here. I might just surprise her one-day. She would have a great time trying to spend all my money." He laughed again as he went on down the aisle to his seat.

As the train pulled out of the station we waved to the family as we moved on down the rails and out of town into the beautiful countryside. There was Josh and Carolyn's ranch to the west of the tracks. We could see all his wonderful horses running along the fence line as the whistle sounded as we passed the crossing that led to the main house that had been built when I was a little boy. I told Josie about working with Josh and how he taught me about raising horses when I was young and when I worked for Foster in his saddle shop. Then she looked at me with those big blue eyes.

"It's so good how you were brought up knowing near everyone in this town and with family with you all your life. That's what I always longed for when I was growing up with just my Aunt."

"I'm sorry Josie didn't mean to make you sad."

"No, BJ I like looking out and imagining how it was in the old days before Durango became so big compared to what it was."

"When pa first came to town there was just one Main Street and Bill Gills worked at the bank just part-time and looking forward to being a lawyer one day. Now look at him and Mr. Winslow was just a small banker trying to get by."

As we talked and looked out the window the morning passed as we went pass Chimney Rock and we were coming into Pagosa Springs before we knew it was near and this was our first stop to pick up more passengers. The conductor yelled.

"You'll have one hour to look around. So be on your toes and get back for we wait for no one."

We left the train but there wasn't much to see except wonderful colored boulders around the town.

"You know Josie looking at these rocks I'm thinking we'll have some story to tell our children one day about how we met down in that Grand Canyon." Josie turned red when she thought of that day down in the canyon.

"Don't remind me I was yelling at Buck and you pretty hard. I was so angry that the beauty of that place was missed. We'll have to go back one day."

We had to scoot back to the train and when we came near Josie pulled at my sleeve.

"BJ look at that man getting on the train. The one with his hat pulled down low and his gun hanging low down."

"What of it?"

"I bet my last dollar that he's one of Uncle Martin's men."

"He couldn't be they were all rounded up at the mine or the shoot out on the road outside of town."

"I don't know. Don't take your wallet out I know how they work. He's trying to see who has what as he walks up and down."

Josie turned quiet during the next leg of the trip and kept watching that man as he walked up and down the aisle as we moved to our next stop. In Saguache Josie spotted another man that she knew. In Fair Play and Bailey the same thing happened now four men were on the train that Josie thought she knew. Two of the men had gone to the second passenger car. When we came to our stop in Denver Josie wanted to wait to see if the four men got off. As the men were getting off one of them stopped in front of us and tipped his hat in our direction.

"Nice to see you again young lady." Then he left as I started to raise and go after him but Josie held me back and said.

"Let it pass for now. We'll just wait and see what happens on the return trip."

We came to the hotel and checked in and were taken down a plush hallway that looked to be lined with carpet even on the walls. As the door opened we saw the most elegant room in the country to my eyes.

"Your father booked us the honeymoon suite. Look at the heart shaped pillows on the couch and the bed and look here a bucket with champagne." The bellboy put down our luggage and Josie's trunk came rolling in the door on a two-wheel dolly.

"Yes ma'am this is the best room in the hotel and if you need anything just pick up the phone and tell them what you want and I'll come running day or night. I'm assigned to you until you leave."

I reached in my pocket to pull out a ten-dollar bill and he put up his hand to stop me.

"It's been taken care of sir. We know Silver Buck around here and he paid for everything you might need. Just ask for Justin and I'll be here." As Justin left he looked at us and said.

"You two have fun now." We both laughed and Josie covered up her red face as Justin walked out the door.

The days in Denver were full of site seeing and a trip was taken by me to the stockyards as Josie spent an afternoon shopping in a most fashionable side of town. That was the only time we were apart during our honeymoon. She didn't mine the cows at home cause they were spread out over a few thousand acres of land but here they were to confined and smelled terrible to her sense of smell. To me buying clothes was going in picking out some durable clothes and leave but not to a woman, I found out, the idea was to pick what was in fashion at the time in New York or Chicago or in that part of town in Paris, in the right color and not a size to big or small to make you look as though you were born to wear the clothes that you picked. In Durango I had no clue about where she would wear them. I loved to see her in a pair of jeans and one of my shirts that fit her so snug riding her horse with the wind blowing through her long red hair. I guess that was just a man's point of view. We ate out at all different types of restaurants that were about town and she did wear those fancy dresses and even got me in a men's clothes store and had me well fixed with two suits. I insisted they had to be suits of the western style and not like was worn in New York or Paris. Had to have a new hat and boots. I told her that Foster would be upset for he was also a fine western boot maker. But I gave in and would have Foster make me another pair later. That was most of our days in Denver but the nights were filled with love and bliss late into the night. I now understood why my father loved my mother so much. We only called on Justin when we wanted a late-night snack.

Two nights before we were to hop the train for home we were out at a local restaurant that we had been back to a few time cause we were treated politely and the food was of our liking. For some reason on this night I had unpacked my bullwhip and had it across my left shoulder down to my waist on the right side of my body. Josie thought it unfashionable for Denver for what could happen in a city as this. I also had looked closely at my gun and holster but decided to only take the whip that was enough protection. As we were coming out of the door of that restaurant and walking two blocks to our hotel there came out of a dark alley three men wearing side arms but only one had his gun drawn. He looked at us as he came out of the shadows as we stop still in our tracks. He made a strange comment for a thief.

"Hey Josie, it's good to know that you enjoyed your honeymoon but now it's time for your wealthy husband to hand over some of the wealth to your uncles old comrades."

"I thought I recognized you three from the train. Now I know why. You gave up the big jobs and just are concentrating on the small stuff."

"You know a man has to make a living and a little something on the side never hurt. Now hand it over sonny, my boy."

I acted nervous as I took out my new wallet, that Josie had bought me before we left Durango from Foster's shop and threw it in the air toward the man with the gun. As the wallet flew through the air all three of the men's attention was diverted to the wallet in the night air. As they were watching to catch my wallet I grabbed the handle of my black bullwhip and it sliced its way through the thin air and caught the gun barrel and wrist of the man and brought his gun back to my other hand and as I pointed it at the three and cracked the bullwhip in the air again to land around the neck of one of the other men and he was pulled off his feet to the hard wet ground as the first man with the gun was holding his wrist that caught the brunt of the blow so I threw a few words of my own their way.

"Now I think that you three should get lost in the dark."

The third man had already seen the light and had turned and ran down the dark alley and the others got to their feet and limped away in the same direction. I heard as they limped away.

"You'll get yours sonny one of these days. Just you wait till you're on the train. You'll see."

I turned and looked at Josie as I unloaded his gun and tossed it in a trashcan down the street and picked up my wallet lying in the middle of the street as we walked toward our hotel.

"Wonder what that meant."

"No idea, but we better stay on our toes all the way home. You know dear that just felt so good and came out so naturally."

"What did?"

"Home!"

We laughed all the way to the hotel arm in arm. Then the next morning we order breakfast in our room and when Justin brought the tray in he told us.

"It has been a real pleasure to serve you two. For a son of a rich man you aren't like the others always demanding things to be done their way."

"Justin, that's cause I work hard as one of the cowboys on our ranch and know what a hard day's work is. My father and mother have raised all their children like that. We have always had a nice house but I never thought of my family being rich and no better than anyone else in this world. I like you very much and if you lived in Durango we would probably be friends."

"You are one of a kind and I wish you two all the luck throughout your life. I might even show up one day in your town. Who knows what might happen in the future, I'm kind of tired of this job."

In the morning we started packing but Josie found that she had bought so much that we were going to need another trunk. Off we went in search of another trunk in the streets of Denver with never a thought of the night before. The walks were packed with people going places and the streets were full with horses and buggy's going down the now cobblestone streets but only a few were done this way the branches off main were still the dirt and dust of old times. We found the trunk and had it delivered to our room at the hotel and eat dinner at our favorite restaurant and headed back to the hotel. Dusk was coming on in the west and the view of the mountains was spectacular but the buildings left spots that left the mountains somewhat hidden at some points. As we neared the hotel Josie pointed out a man looking our way on the corner of the hotel as he was mounting his horse and galloped away around the corner of the hotel.

"BJ I swear that is one of the men from last night. You think they know where we've been staying."

"Could be but I didn't see much of the other two as I was staring down the barrel of a .45. That kind of keeps your attention."

We were on our way up to our room but we had not seen Justin. He was always there to greet us when we came back from a site seeing trip.

At the top of the stairs there were people crowding the hallway as we pushed aside people to work our way to the room at the end of the hall. We saw as we reach our room the door was open and men were coming out into the hall. As we entered our room there on the floor was Justin sitting up rubbing his head.

"You all right Justin. What happened?"

"I was coming to your room to check to make sure everything was perfect for your last night here. I saw your door was open just a little and I knew you were out so I opened the door slowly and saw that the room had been torn apart as you can see."

As I helped Justin up and supported him for he was still a little woozy on his feet Josie and me had a glance around and saw our clothes out of our suitcases scattered all around the room. Some were torn to bits, as they had to be looking for something. Justin was still talking as I guided him to a chair to sit down.

"Whoever it was hit me on the head as I came in and started to close the door. My lights didn't go out as I watched him go through my pockets as another man came from the bedroom and looked at me."

"That's not him he doesn't have Josie with him. It's not here he must have it on him let's get out of here." They left me laying here and the door open. They must know you from somewhere because they called Mrs. Taylor by her first name."

"You were lucky cause we met them last night near a dark alley."

As Justin walked out under his own power we noticed the new trunk was there opened but not hurt next to our other one that had already been packed but now was empty with the contents all over the room. We spent most of the night packing all over again and then we undressed and fell into bed all worn out.

The next morning we were refreshed as we sat in the tub washing each other's backs but Josie was very quiet. I asked her.

"What's wrong?"

"Oh nothing." Then she went on. "Last night Justin called me Mrs. Taylor and it struck me that was the first time that anyone has called me Mrs. Taylor since the wedding and it felt good in my mind."

As we were drying each other off I told her.

"With all that happened last night that's what stuck in your mind this morning."

"Yes, she said with a giggle in her voice."

There was a knock on the door as we hurried to get our bathrobes on and I went to the door. I looked through the keyhole just to make sure who it was. I saw it was Justin as I open the door and three men came in with him.

"We'll take your luggage to the station and make sure it gets on board so you won't have to worry about anything. The manager said he is so sorry about what happen last night and the police were notified and are looking for the two men."

Josie stuck her head out the bedroom door.

"Hello Justin. How's the head this morning?"

"Still there and working but a big knot on the back. Thanks for caring Mrs. Taylor."

"Now you listen Justin. I love my new name but all our friends call me Josie and he's BJ and you are our friend. Now get out so we can get dressed and make the train on time."

"Yes ma'am. I never had anyone call me friend that stayed here. You're already checked out just leave the key on the dresser and the maid will pick it up."

They took all our luggage and we dressed fast and went out the front door of the hotel where the doorman already had a buggy waiting for us and we were on our way to the train and home.

The train was crowed as we worked our way down the aisle to our seats. As we reached our seats we had a great surprise waiting us as we sat down cause there sitting in front of us was Justin with an eastern hat sitting on his head and an eastern suit with a bowtie around his neck and a large smile from ear to ear on his face. We just stared with our mouths wide open. As we came to our senses I asked.

"What are you doing here Justin?"

Justin looked at us and the smile was gone from his face and he looked so forlorn as we listen to his story.

"We have time for my story. You see I was born in New York City and grew up poor and one day when I was about sixteen I saw a fancy hotel on 5th Avenue. There was an older boy my age running out of the front door with luggage and a well-to-do man and his lady coming out behind him. He put their luggage in a waiting carriage and they left after handing him some money. He went back inside. I asked the doorman what that boy was doing. He told me he was a bellmen and carried people luggage from their room to a waiting carriage or the other way. But he said you would have to dress nice to get a good job like that. I only had my one old shirt and pants. But I was determined and I started to shine men's shoes with the shoe shining box I bought with the couple of dollars I had saved. I shined shoe from 5th Avenue to Broadway in front of the theaters. For six months I did this until I was sick of looking at shoes. I bought my first suit and went to get me that good paying job. The doorman said as I was walking in the door.

"Good going son, Good luck." That made me feel great as I walked up to the manager of the hotel but he said they didn't need anyone. I was depressed but as I walked out the doorman called me over.

"My names Tom, I knew we didn't need a bellmen but wanted to see you when he said no. You look so sad and put out but you can't let that stop you for one minute. You go down the street and go into every hotel with a smile on your face, you know they like that in the hotel business, and I know before the days out a nice looking kid like you will have a job." So I did and had a job in no time. They gave me a uniform and I began to make lots of tips. As a young kid I read about the west so after two years I had enough to take the train to Denver. Most of my money went to my folks to buy food for my younger brother and sister. I wanted to work on a ranch or out in the mountains that looked so stately but again no one would hire a eighteen-year-old kid from New York wearing this here suit. I had to eat and my money ran out I did what I knew how to do. I got the job at the Denver Hotel and have been there for a year. When I talked to you that old feeling came over me. When you two said this morning that I was truly your friend I just had to come to Durango."

"That's some story but that suit will never do in Durango even the hotel clerk don't wear anything that nice and that hat will have to go."

"You're not mad."

Josie spoke as she looked at Justin.

"As I said you're our friend and we'll help you fit in and do something you like to do."

He sat back and relaxed looking out the window and then he turn to look back.

"See that man three seats back. I never forget a face, in my business it does one good to remember names and faces, and that is one of the men that torn up your room last night and there is the other one two seats in back of him."

We looked and sure enough they were the same two in front of the restaurant. We looked around more and the third man was in our sight but in the opposite direction. We were in between the three and there may be more throughout the train car. Josie looked for more and she looked at Justin and me.

"I know those three and I see two more from my uncle's gang. Justin, get ready for a shock. I lived with my uncle out here after my aunt died in Boston. He was the leader of a gang of Comancheros. He's died now but BJ and his friends saved me. These are some that must have escape."

Justin turned blue around the mouth.

I had packed my guns and whip in the trunk and that trunk was three cars back with all the baggage.

"We'll just have to hope for the best. We should be home tomorrow noon."

As we headed southwest passengers left the train at Bailey and more at Fair Play and as the train moved into the night we stopped at Saguache for an hour and we went through the station and hurried with Justin right behind us. I found what I was looking for a gun shop. I bought a small derringer that I could hide just in case of trouble and a box of shells. I loaded it and put it in my inside pocket of my suit. We jumped on board just as the train pulled out of the station. Most people were asleep as we moved down the track into the dark stary night. In the morning we came to Pagosa Springs. Here most of the passengers got off and there were only eight people left in our car besides us, there were five men and three were the ones from Denver the other two Josie knew. They were all armed. The conductor came in our car and was just walking through as one of the men grabbed the conductor around the throat and drew his gun and put it to the conductor's head. I jumped up and drew the gun I had bought when a gun came down on my head from behind and Josie yelled and Justin try to help but was knocked back into his seat and a fourth man put a gun to his head.

Josie turned as a voice spoke to her from behind as she bent down to see about me as I was rubbing my head.

"Hello Josie. How you been? It's been a long time."

"What you mean Bert there's no Comancheros left to back you up my uncle's dead."

"These four is all I need for now. We're all that's left of Martin's Comancheros. We'll get more later."

Bert had a paper in his other hand the one without the .45 in it. He handed it to the conductor as Bert pulled the cord to stop the train. The train came to a screeching halt right outside of town as everyone held on to the seat trying not to fall. I was up on my feet now and put my hat back on my head.

"Lance, take the conductor to tell the engineer and fireman to get this train on that siding just outside of town. Then you conductor take that note to the Sheriff, he'll know what to do with it. Lance stay with the engineer to make sure there's no funny business going on. Everyone just sit down and don't get any funny ideas. Jerry, you and Sid get in the other car and disarm everyone, search the ladies to."

I sat down with Josie beside me and Justin looked pale and nervous sitting across from us as I told Bert.

"What you hope to do with us and what's that note for?"

"You'll find out when your rich daddy brings the money. Silver Buck just hit it rich again. It was in the Denver paper."

The train started to move again slowly down the track and made a jog to the right off the main track then came to a halt. It was an hour before the conductor came back.

"Well, what he say? What's your name anyway?

"Ben, and Gus the sheriff went straight to the telegraph office and sent the message that you gave me. Said he'll come with an answer when it comes."

"What took you so long?"

"He wasn't in his office the deputy had to go find him. He came running when he saw the train stopping then pull off the main track."

"Alright now sit and we wait."

Justin was holding his head in his lap and was making all kinds of noise as Bert went straight to him.

"Say you shut up or I'll make you so you don't cry anymore."

That didn't help at all as Justin just kept crying as the people of Pagosa Springs gather outside to see what was going on. Sid came in with an arm full of weapons and dropped them in the corner by the stove way out of our reach. Bert told Sid.

"Take this blubbing idiot to the baggage car and lock him in there. I'm tired of hearing him."

Justin bent over crying and Josie and me bent down to help him in the other seat. We were surprised when he spoke low to us.

"Pretend with me. I have an idea, be prepared when I come back." Then he started carrying on again and Sid grabbed his arm and pulled him up out of his seat and shoved him down the aisle with a gun pointed in his back as they left the car. Josie and me just looked at each other dumbfounded. She shrugged her shoulders with a puzzled look on her face as I had the same look on mine so we got up and sat in our seats again.

"That's much better peace and quiet at last."

"You don't know my father he'll hunt you down to the ends of the earth before he'll give you any undeserved money. He has partners that will help him hunt you down and one of them wears a badge."

"You just wait and see. He will or he'll have a dead son and daughter-in-law on his hands."

"Have you thought this out if we're dead then you'll be dead soon after and won't have any money?"

****

17

Chad came running and threw open the door of the Sheriff's office completely out of breath with a telegram in his hand. John had been sitting in his office chair turned away from his desk and the door cleaning his rifle when Chad rushed in.

He jumped out of his chair and turned toward the open door with the rifle in his hand and caught Chad as he stumbled to him.

"Take it easy Chad my boy. What is it?"

Chad was so out of breath that he couldn't speak but held out the telegram for John to take. As John read Chad got his breath back enough to say.

"They have BJ and want money or kill them."

"Chad, listen to me. Get Foster and find Tim and Bill at their offices. Tell them to ride to the ranch as fast as they can."

John took his hat off the rack and tucked the telegram in his pocket. His horse was always tied in front of his office ready to go at a minutes notice during the day as he untied him and jumped in the saddle and galloped out of town. Foster was in the front of his store when John passed by.

"What's you'se in a rush for John?"

"Ask Chad, I'm going to the ranch."

Foster looked around and spotted Chad coming out of Bill's office with Bill and Tim at his heels as they came toward him.

"The Sheriff wants you at the ranch as soon as possible. They have BJ and Josie."

The three mounded and were on their way with not a sound between them except of the hoofs of the horses beating at the dirt as they left Durango behind. As they reached the ranch the front of the house was already full of mounted men with Buck in the led. Red Bird was dressed for riding and was up on Lagger as she yelled to Molly.

"Take care of the children we'll bring them back safe never you worry."

Buck saw Foster and Bill with Tim. He threw the telegram to them as the men were riding out of the gate for a two-day ride. Buck yelled at Bill.

"Get the money from the bank and follow us just in case. Send a telegram back to Pagosa Springs and let them know we are on our way with the money. It will take two days to get there."

Bill looked at the telegram and read $50,000 dollars or your son and Josie are dead. Bill rode as fast as he could to the bank as Foster and Tim followed.

The two-day trip was going to be grueling. Manuel and Juan had packed food for ten men for four days in the saddlebags that every horse had on its back and enough lead to support a small army. They stopped late into the first night and three fires were going as the men ate and the horses rested by the stream. Red Bird was beside herself as she paced up and down. Buck went to her and held her as she started to cry.

"They have my oldest and we have to get them back and destroy the men that have them. The west was supposed to be different now."

"Red Bird, don't worry we'll get them out safe and sound and the west is changing but there are those that want to live in the old ways but it won't last. Now get some rest."

******

"I know they're here somewhere." Justin kept going through the baggage looking for the Taylor's trunks that were here in the baggage car. The fake tears were gone now as Justin kept looking. It was getting late into the night but that would not stop him. He knew he could help his new friends if he could just fine what he was looking for. It had to be near morning when he turned over a tarp in the corner of the car and there they both were. He opened the first one and it was all Josie's new dresses and the second was Josie's also. He pulled the trunks aside and there was a large suitcase and then he spotted the saddlebags that he had seen on the bed the night before they left. He usually didn't touch guess things but this was life and death and he didn't work for the hotel anymore so he unbuckled the saddlebags and there was what he had seen laying on the bed beside a suitcase. Justin reached in and pulled out BJ's gun and his bullwhip. He looked at them in admiration as he had on that night in their hotel room.

He had to think of a way to get these to BJ. He had never picked up a gun and he had just read stories about what a bullwhip would do to a man. He picked up the gun and saw some ammunition and raised the suit coat in the back and stuck the gun in his pants under his coat and put some ammunition in his coat pockets. He saw a smaller suitcase and open it to see some men's clothes which he dumped in back of the trunk and put the bullwhip in the bottom. He opened Josie's trunk with some dresses and split skirts for riding and threw these things on top of the whip with a comb and brush then some perfume that smelled delightful. Now he tucked the dresses around the bullwhip and hoped they would hide the whip until Josie got hold of the suitcase. He was ready now if only he could get back in the passenger car. Justin looked through the cracks in the wall of the train and saw that it was late in the day. For how long before dark he did not know. There was a noise outside the door so he laid down and pretended to be asleep. The door opened and Jerry was standing in the doorway looking down at him. He could feel BJ's gun poking him in the back as he sat up and rubbed his eyes as he raised his head off the suitcase.

"I see you calmed down."

"I just never was knocked around like that and a gun put in my face. It was just unnerving. I'm alright now."

"That's good cause the boss wants us all together when the money comes later."

He had his gun out and was motioning for Justin to go out the door. He rose and picked up the suitcase and Jerry said.

"What you doing with that put it down."

"It's just some things that I thought Josie might need in the morning. Hair brush and comb and a couple of fresh dresses for her to change into when we leave."

"Who said you're leaving, let me have a look inside."

"When Bert gets the money he'll let us go. Right!"

Jerry said as he opened the suitcase and sweat broke out on Justin's face as Jerry looked inside and pushed the dresses to the side and as he watched Jerry the whip stayed hidden.

"It seems alright but I don't know if Bart is going to let her go. He might keep her for our pleasure. Her uncle's not around now to stop us."

"Anyway she would like to freshen up." Justin said as Jerry closed the lid and locked the latches. He motioned for me to go to the other car. Justin picked up the suitcase and had it held in his two arms as they entered the passenger car. Bert halted Justin and asked Jerry. "What's this?"

"I checked it. Just some dresses for Josie and her brush and comb."

"Well I say. It might be nice to watch her change while we're waiting."

BJ jumped up but Sid knocked him down to his knees and Josie was right by his side. BJ looked up into Bart's eyes.

"I'll see you in hell if you ever touch my wife."

Justin put the suitcase beside Josie and told her.

"There's perfume in the "bottom". Have a look Mrs. Taylor."

"I thought we told you to call us by our first names."

"I know it's just out of habit Mrs. Taylor."

Now Josie was suspicious that something was up as she opened the suitcase cause it wasn't her suitcase as she looked in the bottom and saw the edge of the whip.

"Thank you Justin. This is my favorite and my riding skirt to go home wearing."

Josie took Justin's face in her two hands with real excitement in her voice and kissed him on the cheeks as Justin whispered to her.

"Tell BJ to look under the back of my coat. Check my right pocket for more." Bert said.

"That's enough get your husband up in that seat and be still."

Justin saw as they helped BJ to his feet Josie whispered to BJ. They both lifted BJ by his arms and helped him to the seat. As Justin turned to sit down he stopped and turned so his back would be right in front of BJ and spoke to Bert.

"Do you want me to sit here or over there?"

Justin could feel BJ hand go under his coat and in his pocket as he stood still blocking Bert's sight of BJ as he was talking.

"You fool sit where you like. Just don't start acting up again or it might be a bullet to the head this time and off the train you'll fly."

BJ hid the gun by bending over like his stomach hurt. He managed to get a good grip on his gun that was in his lap and when the time was right he would go into action. The sheriff of Pagosa Springs had been trying it get Bert to let the people go all during the day but now he came up close to the train and made one more plea with Bert.

"Let the people go, Silver Buck has telegrammed he's coming with the money by sometime tonight."

"You listen to me sheriff you stay away from this train and keep the people away or all these so-called nice people will die. To show everyone I mean what I say here is some lead to prove it."

Bert pulled the trigger and I saw the sheriff go down and holding his arm as I could see the red stain on his shirt getting larger. Bert's attention was outside the window and that of his men as they were laughing as some of the town's people came rushing up and dragged the sheriff away. This had to be my time as I raised my gun and shot Sid that was holding Josie by the arm and then turned and shot Jerry almost point blank behind me as I turned back toward Bert he already had his gun in his hand and fired but the bullet went high as I fired and knocked his hat from his head as he ducked at the same time. I started to fire again but Bert had grabbed Josie by the wrist and pulled her toward the door to the front of the train. As he pulled Josie out the door I followed when Justin reached in the suitcase and yelled.

"BJ, here's your bullwhip."

He tossed it to me as I went out the door and wrapped it over my shoulder hanging down to my opposite side.

"Take care of those two Justin."

As I entered the second passenger car Bert was already going out the front of the car with a good grip on Josie. The people were down in their seats covering up their heads as I passed. Two cowboys rose up and followed me as I reached the front of the car. I couldn't tell if he had gone in the baggage car or up on top till I heard him yelling to Lance.

"Lance, get this train moving fast. Fireman get those logs in that steamer or I'll kill you when I get to you."

I went up the ladder and as my head came up to the top Bert fired at me and the bullet hit the metal ladder I was on and ricocheted into the car behind us. I looked and he was taking Josie down into the wood bin. The train was now starting to move slowly as the two cowboys and me moved along the top of the car. As we moved toward the wood bin Lance started to fire on us as we had to hit the deck and I started to crawl on my stomach toward Lance. He kept firing wildly till his gun was empty and had to reload. I grained my footing and moved forward. The wind was blowing hard against me as I moved with gun in hand and looking out to the south there in the distant came riders, ten or twelve of them and as I moved and the riders got closer cause they had their horses on a fast pace coming toward the now fast-moving train moving through the pine forest. I could see my father and mother in the lead and moving fast away from the others and closer to us. I had reached the wood bin as Lance had reloaded and as he raised his gun the cowboy shot the gun out of his hand and the gun went flying into the trees along the tracks. As I jumped into the wood bin on top of Lance and knocked him up to the top of the wood where the cowboys had a hold of him as he held his wrist. I glanced and saw father reach the train and jump aboard and pulled mother up off of Lagger. Bert had Josie with one hand around her throat and the other with his gun pointed to her head.

"I'll kill her if you make a move toward me."

It was an automated reflects as Bert was talking my hand felt for the end of the whip and it was in my hand and flying through the air. The whip had wrapped around the barrel of Bert's gun and I yanked back and it went flying to the top of the baggage car as I rushed to him and Josie. I pulled Josie out of Bert's arm and the fireman pushed her down out of the way as I hit Bert square in the face and he went flying in the bin of wood. The train was now slowing as Bert raced pass the two cowboys that were holding on to Lance. I passed them as I went toward Bert as he reached the top of the baggage car and reached for his gun. My whip was in action again as it caught the gun as he raised it toward me and it went flying again out in the free air and down into the valley below as the train was coming to an uphill grade. I reached Bert and hit him again and that's when I saw mother and father come up on top of the car and Bert caught me on the chin and towards the edge and went flying on over the edge of the train out into space. My whip had wrapped around one of the stovepipes and I was hanging down pass the windows of the rail car but I was alive as I started pulling myself up to the top again. When I reached the top I saw pa hit Bert that went flying over my head yelling as he fell a good two hundred feet to land on top of a boulder in the middle of the river we were now passing over. Ma had a hold of my hand pulling me up on top and gave me a big hug and kissed my cheeks with tears in her eyes. Pa came and patted me and hugged my shoulders as Josie came running into my arms.

"That's my son, takin' care of his woman."

We all looked down on the river as the train slowly backed its way down the track. There we saw the last remains of a mad man with his head crush in the dusk of the coming night and saw Lance standing holding his wounded hand.

"Lance you're the one that will be punished for all the wrong doing of that man and Martin's."

"Me, I just followed orders."

"You knew they were wrong."

Coming up on top we saw Justin walking toward us with the breeze flying through his hair. I took hold of his hand and pulled him toward me.

"Ma, Pa, I want you to meet the hero of this whole affair. He is the reason we are here standing in victory. We have to find him a place in our town and our ranch for him to thrive and make a new start. He's our true friend."

"I'm sure don't know how you did it but if BJ says you did then I know you did. We'll talk later son."

When the train reached Pagosa Springs again the sheriff took charge of Lance. We all spend the night in the hotel until morning when we boarded the train and rolled on to Durango. The horses deserved the rest in the livestock car. The rest of the ride home was peaceful as a spring morning with Josie curled up in BJ's lap and Red Bird asleep on my shoulder. The town was as we had left it and the hope of everyone was that this kind of evil would soon be in the past.

A few weeks went by and one night Silver Buck heard the whole story from when the young Taylors had met Justin till the end of the train terror. Buck looked straight at Justin as we all sat in front of Pa and Ma's huge fireplace one late night.

"You really did all that and how do you like the hotel business? By your suit you look if it suits you." We all had a big laugh at Justin's expense.

"Well sir, I did do what BJ has told you but to tell the truth I was truly scared to death but I also knew if I didn't my two new friends may be dead so I made up my mind it had to be done. As for the hotel business I do love but it's not much money to be made as a bellman. I love figures and used to keep the books at the Denver Hotel and dreamed of owning one someday. I'm not a very big man and see now I don't really belong in the ranching business but I would like to learn to use a gun and that bullwhip of BJ's is just amazing."

"Justin, we can help you with both of those and I tell you right now you are a hero and a very big man in my book. You were scared and still went forward to help your friends. That's a full-size man that has the guts to do anything he has a mind to. I have learned that the hotel on Main

Street in Durango is for sell. It's by the bank and beside Ann's dress and gun shop, a prime location for a up and coming young man. The owner is a friend of mine and we have talked throughout the years. He was here when I came to town many years ago. He's retiring and wants to sell the hotel that has grown over all these years that Durango has grown----."

Here Justin stopped me.

"That would be great but I have barely enough to live on myself. Soon that money will be gone even with me living here in the bunkhouse but I do love the men and the smell of the leather and the animal smells in the barn. A hotel I could run I have no doubt but no money to buy."

"Justin, would you be still and close your mouth and let pa talk."

He twisted his lips like a lock was there as Buck started in again.

"Like I was saying, Mr. Baily and me have been friends a long, long time. I will put up the money for you and I know that you will pay me back out of the profits. Now you can talk, Justin."

The look in Justin's eyes were filled with amazement and many thoughts of wonder as he once again opened his mouth to speak when he lost that big smile with a look of amazement now appearing on his face as in his eyes.

"I'm lost for words. You are a true silver of a man. That doesn't come from a hole in the ground. It comes from your golden heart."

"Does that mean we have a deal?"

"Of course and the whole family can stay free any time I have rooms not occupied."

We all laughed as Justin put that big smile back on his face and his two thumbs at the edge of his vest.

"That's a true business man speaking. We'll go in tomorrow and talk with Mr. Baily with Bill along to make out the papers."

"Buck, I forgot to say thank you. I never had anything like this. We were always poor and not much to eat. I started working in a hotel at sixteen and now I'm twenty. I'll always be honest with my customers and if I'm not BJ, you just come after me with that bullwhip of yours and I'll straighten out."

"You will do great just keep that sense of humor with you all the time."

The next day in town Bill was with us when we talked to Mr. Baily. Red Bird had gone to Ann's dress shop to look for a new dress with Josie. Mr. Baily showed Justin around the unoccupied rooms, which there weren't many. We were shown where Justin thought he could live behind the lobby desk there was a large room.

"This is great for one person like me and the kitchen right next door. That's a plus to have a restaurant in the hotel." Buck put in.

"Justin, take that worried look off your face. You can hire kitchen help and waitresses. I already told Bill to give you operating expense for six months." Mr. Baily started in.

"Yes son, the restaurant really does paid for itself and more. I just closed it down a few weeks ago when I decided to retire. I will provide you the names of my employees. They will be so grateful for their job back."

"Thank you Buck and you Mr. Baily."

Bill took charge from here. "It looks like we have a deal. Your selling price was $15,000. I think that these papers will do the job. Justin, I put in the contract that Mr. Baily has a month before you take over. If that's alright."

"It's fine with me." Justin said. Mr. Baily added.

"That's good with me but Justin if you want to come in during that time and start to move in that room and get the restaurant going again feel free to do so. The Mrs.'s and I live down the street."

They shook hands and signed the papers. The deal was set and I thought that Justin would never quit shaking Mr. Baily's hand so hard and thanking him time and again.

We finally got Justin's hand away from Mr. Baily's and Justin said.

"Sorry, I'm just so excited."

Mr. Baily had a big smile on his face.

"I'm glad you're excited that's why I sold it to you. I could see that excitement in your eyes as we looked around. This old girl needs a good hand to guide her into the future. I can tell you will make the hotel what it should be moving into the next century. I know how you feel cause that's how I felt many years ago when I walked in these doors."

As we left Bill turned to me and told us.

"I want you two to take a ride a little ways out of town to the north. I have something to show you out by Josh's ranch."

Red Bird and Josie were in the buggy as we took a nice ride out toward Josh's and when we came up over a small rise there nestled in between the large spruce and evergreens was Josh and Carolyn's house. With the huge barns filled with hay and the large pastures with horses far as the eyes could see. We stopped and looked as Bill had tears come to his eyes.

"Justin, let me tell you about this man next to you and Josie you don't know everything about your new father. He came to this town with not much money. He found out who killed Jeb his great-great-grandfather and then found Jeb's silver mine, which is where he got his name. I was a part-time teller in the bank and wanted to be a lawyer someday. He paid for me to study law and all this horse ranch you see below us is due to his pleasure in helping young people get a good start in life. Same for Sam and Ann."

"Now Bill don't you go getting' carried away like that. I just like to see good people follow their dreams and I have the money to spread around to make that happen."

"You know he even gave Foster, Tim, Jim and Sam a percentage in the mine and even me."

"Bill, Justin doesn't want to hear about all that past."

"Why not." Red Bird put into the conversation. My Buck even paid for me to be taught to speak better English by my friend and Bill's wife Jenny."

"I just think it's important for him to know who's backing him up. Now look over on that ridge coming down the road that runs beside Josh's house. I told you Silver that we are coming into a new century fast."

"Yes, what of it."

"Justin, you see those poles being put up by all those men coming down towards Josh's."

"Yes I see them. That looks like the telephone pole that came into Denver a couple of years ago."

"Exactly, that is just what they are. You have a keen eye. They are on their way to Durango and we will be able to call anywhere in this large country that has telephone lines and talk to people on the other end. The telegram will one day be the thing of the past."

We saw a rider coming toward us and started waving his hat in the air when he saw who was coming. He reined in as he came up.

"Carolyn saw you from the porch and wondered why y'all didn't ride on up."

"We're just explaining to Justin here, you know Justin."

"Just by sight."

"Well then Justin this is Josh owner of the J&C Ranch. His better half is up on the porch there and I bet she has a nice pitcher of tea up on that porch."

"She sure does come on up."

As we were riding up to the house I told Josh.

"This is Justin he just bought the hotel and I was telling him how Silver Buck got most of us old people started years back and about the new telephone line coming into town." Buck put in a small word.

"Y'all know I don't cotton to that name Silver. Sometimes that old codger Foster gets to me. When he gave it to me, I didn't think it would take."

"Silver you know you love that old man as much as you do your own father. But now getting back to the subject the lines are coming to our house before going to town. Take no time for me to call and get orders for horses from far away. Beats the mail right dear." Josh was saying as we walked up the steps and Carolyn was there with a large pitcher of that tea.

"You bet I can order anything I want from that Sears catalog and it will come right to my door. Now we have that mail service. Come on in the house girls let these old men tell that youngster about their young days."

On the porch drinking our tea Bill went on and we all listened.

"Just what I was telling Buck. I ordered phone service for me and for your house Buck, as you don't like Silver, you'll be able to call me or Doc if someone gets hurt on the ranch and take orders for your cattle from up north and they are going to set lines all the way to the mine so if anything happens that far away it will only take minutes to get help coming their way instead of one or two days that it takes now."

"I can see that people can call the hotel and get a room when they are coming to town."

"That's the sprite Justin." Silver Buck added.

"I can see times are changing and to get along we have to make adjustments in our lives. Maybe Red Bird can talk to Dancing Bear in his teepee one day." From the house came a voice that Silver Buck knew very well."

"I hear that Silver Buck Taylor. That would be nice."

All us had a great laugh sitting on the porch drinking tea as the sun passed the noontime and things were great in our neck of the woods.

THE END

Printed in the USA
CPSIA information can be obtained
at www.ICGtesting.com
LVHW101140180823
755120LV00001B/5